CHRIS LOWRY

Battlefield Z Bluegrass Zombie
Print Version August 2023

Copyright © 2023 by Chris Lowry

All rights reserved. No part of this publication may be reproduced, stored or transmitted in any form or by any means, electronic, mechanical, photocopying, recording, scanning, or otherwise without written permission from the publisher. It is illegal to copy this book, post it to a website, or distribute it by any other means without permission.

First edition

This book was professionally typeset on Reedsy. Find out more at reedsy.com

Contents

1	CHAPTER ONE	1
2	CHAPTER TWO	4
3	CHAPTER THREE	7
4	CHAPTER FOUR	11
5	CHAPTER FIVE	15
6	CHAPTER SIX	18
7	CHAPTER SEVEN	22
8	CHAPTER EIGHT	25
9	CHAPTER NINE	31
10	CHAPTER TEN	35
11	CHAPTER ELEVEN	39
12	CHAPTER TWELVE	43
13	CHAPTER THIRTEEN	47
14	CHAPTER FOURTEEN	52
15	CHAPTER FIFTEEN	57
16	CHAPTER SIXTEEN	66
17	CHAPTER SEVENTEEN	69
18	CHAPTER EIGHTEEN	74
19	CHAPTER NINETEEN	81
20	CHAPTER TWENTY	86
21	CHAPTER TWENTY ONE	90
22	CHAPTER TWENTY TWO	97
23	CHAPTER TWENTY THREE	100
24	CHAPTER TWENTY FOUR	103

25	CHAPTER TWENTY FIVE	107
26	CHAPTER TWENTY SIX	110
27	CHAPTER TWENTY SEVEN	115

1

CHAPTER ONE

Flying.

I sat in the passenger seat and watched my son handle the controls of the tiny Cessna like he was a pro.

I suppose he was, though he had only played with a flight simulator on his computer.

But in a world where we had to escape using a plane, he became a pilot by default.

It's not like I could do much, other than hold the yoke, and probably spiral us down to our death into the pine forests below.

They stretched out to the East as we pointed the nose of the plane toward Alabama and my friends at Fort Jasper.

I planned a quick stop there, and sending Byron and his boys out to find more jet fuel so we could keep hopping in the plane toward the East Coast and the refugee camps where my youngest was supposed to be.

The hunt for Bo Bistan, I joked with the Boy and Bem.

All nicknames for the kids, all variations of their names, just with the B from that song.

"Nick, Nick, Bo Bick, Banana Fana Fo Fick," or however it went.

Playing around with them when they were younger, and a decade later, that's all I called them.

"Dad," the Boy nodded out of the side of the plane. "That it?"

We had used the Interstate as a guide as it cut across Mississippi and Alabama, and turned North on 22 when it cut through Birmingham.

We passed over the depot where we had established the camp, and the Boy circled looking for a landing strip.

"Interstate?" I yelled over the roar of the prop.

He nodded, and lined up on a straight section for a landing.

It was five or so miles away from the camp, but after hoofing halfway across the country, five miles would be an easy hour and half hike.

He leveled off the wings, brought the plane in low and then I noticed the sweat on his brow, dripping off the end of his nose and splotching onto his pants.

He was nervous.

They say any landing you can walk away from is a good one, and the Boy squelched onto the empty Interstate, screeching the tires as the plane bounced off the asphalt and slithered to a stop after four hundred yards.

He killed the engine and leaned back in the seat.

"Good work," I told him.

"My first landing," he wiped his forehead. "Make it a little rougher next time," Bem added from the backseat.

"I'll probably get better with practice," he said.

There was hope in his voice, and a little trepidation. I didn't blame him.

We were lucky.

CHAPTER ONE

I'd been up in a couple of Cessna's with experienced flyboys.

The takeoff and landings were the hard part.

We had a wide empty roadway that was mostly flat.

If we had to make due with a grass landing, or dodging stalled cars, the ending might have been different.

"Let's move," I told them as I climbed out.

Those five miles weren't going to hike themselves.

CHAPTER TWO

"The gate's open."

"I see."

"That's not a good sign."

I shot a glance at my daughter and saw the tight grin on her face.

She was nervous and trying hard to mask it with a joke.

"Maybe they think we're barbarians at the gate?"

I suggested.

They didn't laugh.

"No guards," the Boy pointed to the corners of the wall.

He was right.

There should have been two people on the gate, if Brian had followed the instructions I left.

The compound itself, Fort Jasper, was at the end of a dirt road on the edge of a ridge.

It was hard to approach in mass, and protected on the back side by a couple of thousand yards of sloping pine forest.

Even though we reinforced the gate, it should have been

watched at all times, at least to warn the rest inside of what to expect.

The rolling fence was partially open.

The tin walls weren't peppered with bullet holes, so at least we had that.

Whatever happened.

It was time to find out.

"Stay here," I took a step forward and they both followed.

"We're watching your back, Dad."

My heart swelled with pride.

I didn't want to tell them it would be easier if I wasn't watching out for them, in case there were Z inside.

But if there were Zombies outside the walls, that would have me worried too.

Worry was a distraction we couldn't afford.

Better to have them with me so I could keep them safe.

I nodded.

"Stay tight. Eyes up."

They both bunched up on my shoulders, a pace back as we went through the gate.

The compound was empty.

I could tell by the sound, the noise, just that feeling from being inside a vast open space where the only thing you can hear is the wind.

No feeling of being watched.

No feeling of anyone around.

No zombies.

No Brian, Anna, Byron, Hannah, none of the boys.

"Where is everyone?" my Boy whispered.

I searched the walls for a sign.

There was no sign of a fight, no streaks of blood and body

parts left that would have indicated a Z outbreak inside.

"It's like they opened up the gate and walked out," said Bem. "Maybe they didn't expect you back."

"They would have left a note," I said and we headed for the giant building we used as a communal space.

CHAPTER THREE

If there is one thing my divorces taught me is that you can't rely on anyone.

Or anything.

The origin of the story is sad, or at least if I felt like throwing a pity party it would be.

When the second and I decided to split, she got to keep the money, the condo, the new car, and I got the POS sedan.

It wasn't my first stint at being homeless, which I just called being between homes.

I would go to work in the morning, go to the gym for the evening, sit under a streetlight in the park to read until I was tired, then sleep in the backseat.

Then it was back to the gym in the morning for a workout and shower, over to work, and so on.

I had to do this for two months as I saved up meager pieces of my paycheck for a deposit on a new apartment.

It was more about timing than anything.

I'd get the deposit saved, and the soon to be ex would need something for my daughter.

I was a living embodiment of the working poor.

No one to help me.

I asked my Dad for some help at the time.

He said no.

No to moving in with him.

No to a loan.

Then I found out he offered his spare bedroom to a guy he worked with who was down on his luck.

That was the lesson I needed to learn.

No one is going to help you.

The only person who can do anything for you, is you.

And I vowed then to become a guy who can help others when they asked.

Eventually I moved up at my job, I was paid more, had a place to live and went from sleeping in my car to a queen size bed.

I kept moving up in title and income, but I never lost that lesson.

Self-reliance is the only thing that can carry you through sometimes.

No matter what lies you have to tell yourself to get up and keep fighting, it was always a matter of getting after it every day.

Someone told me they felt like they were going through hell because they scheduled their days too busy, had to do dishes after cooking dinner, and had a four thousand square foot house to clean.

I laughed and told them to keep on going.

I didn't share with them that I ate a pouch of tuna sitting on a park bench watching the moon rise over a lake before going to sleep in my car the night before.

Lesson learned.

I just didn't realize I was prepping for the Zombie apocalypse at the time.

"What are you thinking about?" the Boy asked.

I glanced over and saw his eyes shining in the firelight.

Moist.

"You won't remember, but when you were a toddler, we did a lot of camping like this."

"Zombies outside the tent then?" he smirked and wiped the end of his nose with the back of his hand."

There are always wolves out there.

And bears.

And skunks. But I was thinking about the last time I camped withall three of you.""I don't remember."

"We should have done it more. I was thinking about spending more time with you, how I wished I would have."

He adjusted the way he was sitting in the nest of blankets.

"I was thinking about mom," he said just above a whisper.

I almost asked what happened.

But Bem said his name.

Soft too, like a partially warning laced with regret.

"I miss her."

Bem sobbed into a blanket.

And I regretted feeling sorry for me.

Maybe that was one of the sources of my rage, maybe even the main source.

Who was I to throw a pity party for myself when there were other people out there suffering, kids who had it worse than me.

Homeless?

Sure, but I had a tin roof rusting over my head back then and food to eat.

There were dads who had to sleep on the ground.

Sad I didn't spend more time with my children?

My mom had died when I was twenty-one, so I had been alive longer without her than before.

That scar had healed, but it was fresh on Bem and the Boy.

Raw.

They needed to be protected, they needed routine and safety.

I thought we might find it at Fort Jasper, but the empty rooms, the empty walls, the open gate and everyone gone meant it wasn't here.

Even though we didn't know what happened, I needed to skip wondering about my little group of survivors, and focus on the mission.

Get my youngest.

Get these kids someplace safe.

Keep them safe.

Let them heal.

Be the rock they could rely on always.

I rolled up onto my knees and crawled across our little campsite to plop down between them, then reached for both to drag them into an embrace.

They cried against my sides then, the Boy starting and Bem following.

Great heaving sobs that poured their grief, and despair and anger out onto me, dripping like tears across my shirt, soaking the layers.

I may have cried too.

Sad for their loss, and sad for the loss of a woman I loved once.

And maybe for what I had lost again.

There was too much gone in this new world.

CHAPTER FOUR

"Someone's coming."

The Boy lifted his rifle and sighted on movement in the woods.

I moved away from the kids and out in the open from the shadows to be a target and draw focus on me.

"Stay back," I said out of the corner of my mouth.

"I got him Dad," the Boy said, a hint of exasperation coloring his voice.

I wondered for a second if he thought I was being too overprotective, then decided I didn't care.

Since I found them, we had been captured, chased, shot and left for Z food in the middle of a football field.

I didn't think I was bad luck for the kids, but the reason behind our string of bad situations was my fault.

It's not every day you get to piss off an insane militia man masquerading as a General, who declares a personal vendetta against you and chases you halfway across the country.

I was sure we had lost them by stealing an airplane from Vicksburg and flying East.

But if there was one thing I had learned in the zombie Armageddon was to always expect the unexpected.

Which is why I smiled when Tyler stepped out of the trees.

"You were making a lot of noise," I lowered the rifle and reached out to shake his hand.

"I wanted you to know it was me," he cradled a hunting rifle in the crook of his arms, bundled up in layers of long sleeves, long pants and a hunting poncho.

He had a branch with leaves stuck in the straps of his pack, a moving piece of shrubbery,and the coloring of his clothing meant he had to work to make sure we saw him.

"Where is everyone?"

He stared at the gate over my shoulder.

"I've been out a week," he said and shrugged.

Tyler was somewhere between fifteen and seventeen, small boned, razor thin made more so by hunting and scavenging to survive.

He was also one of the best woodsmen I had ever seen, skills honed to a sharp edge by constant use since the Z came.

"Place is empty," I informed him. "No sign of struggle."

He took it well, and stepped past me to inspect the interior of Fort Jasper.

I watched him stutter step as he caught sight of Bem, a typical teen boy reaction, despite her lumpy clothes and shapeless jacket.

I had a mini-war of pride and protectionist because my girl was still quite beautiful even under layers of dirt, grime and looking like homeless person.

Say what you will about everything else I've done wrong in the world, I made gorgeous babies.

I started to clear my throat and noticed the Boy glaring too.

He was taking being an overprotective brother seriously, so my pride swelled again.

Tyler recovered and marched through the gate.

Bem played with a strand of hair and tucked it behind her ear.

I decided to let it, followed the teen into the compound, and watched as he cast around quickly and came back to stand in front of me.

"No struggle," he said. "No blood."

"No Z."

He shook his head and studied the ground.

"Rain a couple of days ago cleaned up the dirt. Let's look outside."

"Gear up," I told the Boy.

He glared at Tyler and began to clear out our little campsite from the previous night.

Bem and I trailed Tyler as he made ever widening circles from the gate to the road, searching for signs of passage.

"Got something," he waved me over.

Boot prints under overturned leaves, pointing away from the compound.

"We could have figured that out since there's only one way to go," the Boy snarled as he caught up, huffing under the weight of three packs.

He passed one to Bem, the other to me and adjusted the one he had on his back.

Tyler shot him a look and nodded, biting back any comment he might have made.

"Shut the gate?" Bem pointed.

Our scout watched her move toward the gate and kept watching as she pulled it closed.

"Where to next?" the Boy brought his attention back to the

ground.

We fell in line behind Tyler as he moved to the main road.

"No tire tracks yet," he said. "Still walking."

He pointed to scuffed tracks in the dirt, more than a few, all moving in the same direction.

There wasn't much more to see, but we walked on the blacktop as he tracked whatever happened, our eyes and ears listening for zombies, and anything else that seemed out of place.

The Boy watched Tyler, as he kept glancing at Bem out of the corner of his eyes, and she blushed when he caught her staring.

I sighed.

Human nature didn't give a damn about the zombie plague.

CHAPTER FIVE

We hit the railroad tracks and still hadn't found anything.

Just boot prints on the side of the road, all headed in the same direction.

Scuff marks in the leaves, overturned twigs and branches.

Sign of a large group passing through, normal walking patterns according to Tyler so not zombies, but nothing more.

"Where are they going?" I wondered aloud.

"If it's even our group."

I hadn't considered that.

What if we were on the wrong trail?

What if it wasn't Anna or Brian or the others, but some marauders or bandits that came along after.

"Tracks," I said.

"Where?" the Boy searched the ground.

"Train tracks," I pointed. "We're going to follow them."

Tyler studied the ground on either side of the rails.

"They did not go that away," he smirked.

"We are," I told them.

"We don't know who we're following. Or what. But I do know where we need to go."

"Find the others," Tyler said.

"If we can. But we're going to have to rely on luck a little for that. Right now, we need the essentials. Food. Shelter. More weapons. The rail is easy to follow."

"Keeps us elevated on a slope," Tyler appraised the terrain.

"We haven't seen many of the Z, Dad."

The Boy was right.

We hadn't heard any moaning, or groaning or seen the shuffle of a gray skinned body filter through the trees.

I held up my hand for quiet and we listened to the birds in the trees.

Nature sounded normal.

"Are we going in the right direction?" Bem asked.

It was the first time she spoke on our hike and Tyler quirked his head to one side like he had heard a Siren calling him to the rocks.

I almost punched him back to reality but took a breath instead.

"East," I told her. "Somewhere up there is Fort Knox."

"You want gold Dad?"

"All of it in the world Boy," I clapped him on the shoulder. "We'll build thick walls from the bars.

But I was thinking an Army base would have maps of the refugee centers and that's the only one I know about.

"I shot a look at Tyler and he made a face, shook his head no.

He didn't know of any others either.

Which made sense.

Neither of us were from Alabama.

He was a Georgia kid picked up from a Children's Brigade I ran across in my race across the deep South.

And I'd never had cause to know much about anything North of the interstate in Alabama.

It was all fresh territory for us.

"If we find another depot, or base we can check, but we'll make our way east and North until then."

"Kentucky is a long walk.

"I sent up a silent prayer to the education gods.

At least the Boy knew Fort Knox was in Kentucky.

"Food first," I laid out the order.

"We could go back for the plane."

The plane would cut our time down and we could search from the air.

I wasn't sure how it would go from the sky though.

It was easy when we were following the interstate, and flying East would make sense.

"If we find fuel and a destination, it might make sense," I agreed with my son.

"But I don't want to run out of gas at five thousand feet."

I didn't wait for them to agree or to offer an opinion.

I just turned and started walking up the middle of the tracks, my steps long enough to hit every other tie between the rails.

They fell in step behind me, Tyler bringing up the rear, and the Boy making damn sure he was between the teen and his sister.

I couldn't keep a grin off my face as we marched through the morning sun.

CHAPTER SIX

"What is that?"

"It's a truck," Bem answered before I could.

We stood between the railway iron in a casual line looking at the crew cab contraption blocking the path in front of us.

It was a regular four door pick up truck, white with the logo of the railroad on it, but with something extra.

"What's wrong with the wheels?" asked the Boy.

It was my fault really.

I missed out on part of his education.

Growing up in Pine Bluff, a small town that sprouted up as a railroad connection to the Arkansas River I sometimes didn't know what they did not know.

Like what a rail truck was.

The regular pick up had been modified with steel wheels that dropped down and locked into position on the rail line.

The wheels would turn the steel, and convert the road driving vehicle into a rail car.

"It's a rail car!" Bem shouted then put a hand over her mouth at the outburst.

That made us all laugh.

Tyler made a big show of it, being sure she saw his appreciation for her joke.

I made a note to pull him aside and do some Dad threats later.

"Exactly," I said.

It was pointed in the right direction, and I wondered why it was out here in the middle of nowhere.

At least until we drew even with the windows.

They were smeared on the inside with gunk and gore.

"Something's in there," said Tyler.

He backed away and pulled his rifle out.

"Too much noise," I said and knocked against the glass.

A Z face bounced off the window trying to snap my fingers off.

Someone died in the truck, a man by the look of what was left and the Z he became was too dumb to get out.

I tried the handle.

It was unlocked.

"Get a branch," I wished for my big giant Bowie knife or a pike instead.

The Boy found a good long, thick branch and I hauled the door open to let the Z out.

A wave of rotting stench washed out with it as the zombie fell out of the door and spilled large puddle of goo onto the cinder bed of the railway.

Bem squeaked and took a step back, slipped and plopped onto her bottom on the tracks.

The movement drew the Z and it slithered toward her, using its arms to drag and leap across the iron rail.

I used the branch as a club and tee'd off on its head, trying for a long hard drive to an imaginary green par four away.

Golf was never my sport, but it was a decent swing if I do say so myself and the Z appreciated it.

His went splat, separated from his neck and bounced down the slope on the side of the railroad.

"Gross," Bem got up and dusted herself off.

"You think that's bad?" the Boy stuck his head in the truck and pulled back out gagging.

I had to agree with him.

Rotting Z stuck in a closed cab since who knew how long, combined with sun and closed windows made for a unique smell combination that sent all of us almost reeling.

"Is this a good idea?" Tyler regained his composure first, but he was the furthest away.

I opened all of the doors, and was glad we were light on breakfast and lunch because there was nothing to bring up.

Zombie apocalypse, not only a great diet opportunity but constant ab workout from dry heaves.

We used pine needles to scrub out the seats and covered the floorboard with fresh ones we pulled from the trees in an effort to mask the smell.

I checked the engine and it turned over, and small luck, the gas gauge said the tank was full.

We turned the A/C on full blast, and stuffed the vents with more needles to fill the cabin with better smell.

"Mount up," I said when I thought it was as good as it was going to get for now.

We would keep the windows down and a breeze blowing through would help.

"Can I drive?" Bem eyed the wheel.

Teens and human nature.

But if you can't learn to drive after the Dead start walking, then when is there a good time.

I motioned her behind the wheel, and slid into the passenger seat as Tyler and the Boy jockeyed for position in back.

She gripped the wheel with both hands and went through the motions of adjusting her mirrors and seat.

"We're the only ones out here and you're locked on a rail," the Boy teased.

"Just press the gas.

"And she did.

CHAPTER SEVEN

Windows down, wind in my hair, the only thing missing was the radio.

It reminded me of rolling through the backroads of Arkansas, only straighter as the rail bed cut through the low rolling hills of North Alabama and cut through Tennessee.

I felt happy.

Two kids with me, a good soldier at our backs, and a full tank of gas to get us closer to our destination.

Then I felt guilty for feeling content, because there was a little girl out there waiting for me to find her.

Waiting for me to rescue her.

Maybe more people waiting on me.

Not that they knew I would come, the rational side of my head tried to argue.

But maybe they hoped I would.

They hoped anyone would I didn't know what kind of trouble moved Brian from his dream Fort.

I wasn't sure why Anna would disappear or where Byron would

take Hannah.

There were too many variables and speculation only led to frustration.

The same with my daughter.

Speculating about fate, about her well being or state of mind would drive me out of mine.

Better to make a plan.

Follow the plan.

There was a map of the refugee centers in Aniston.

Lost now.

But where there was one, there were a hundred spread out on bases across the South.

The Army did nothing in small measures, and what they did print was in triplicate.

We would get our bearings, get a destination and hunt.

I'd find her.

No doubt about it.

I couldn't afford doubt.

It would make me quit and I couldn't quit.

Not ever.

"Slow down," I told Bem as we approached a road.

She pressed the brakes and we were rewarded with a small town a few hundred yards up the road from the railway crossing.

"Anyone feel like shopping?" Bem pressed the parking brake and we got out."

"Do I lock it?"

I almost said no.

But call it a gut feeling.

We were being watched.

By Z or by human I couldn't know yet.

I nodded.

"Seal it tight."

""It's going to stink," Tyler grumbled.

But he closed a window as the Boy rolled up the other.

We clicked the locks shut and grabbed our packs and rifles.

"Eyes up," I told them. "I don't know what's out there but they know we're here."

Bem pocketed the keys and we took off to see what was left of the little map dot the railroad forgot.

CHAPTER EIGHT

We moved from the truck toward the town.

It wasn't a far walk.

I couldn't tell what state we were in yet, the absence of signs on the side of the railroad making it hard to determine location.

But this little berg looked like a hundred others I'd driven through before the Z plague or walked through after.

A main strip that led across the railroad that served as a Broadway, a boulevard and strip mall all at the same time.

Two rows of buildings on either side, a brick two story courthouse from right after World War II, block style with little panache.

Houses beyond the strip, and trailers in the backyard of almost every one of them.

The weeds on the sides of the road were high, overgrown, nature looking to take back what man carved out.

"It's quiet," said the Boy.

I glanced over at his wide eyes roaming from building to building.

He was right.

The insect hum here was gone, the birds quiet.

"Maybe we should go back to the truck," said Bem.

Tyler just clicked the safety off his rifle.

I steered us to the side of the road instead of the center, hand on my rifle, finger off the trigger.

"Let me move ahead," I said over my shoulder.

The kids slowed their pace.

I could hear two sets of footprints and looked back.

Tyler had stopped, moved into the grass and was aiming at the rooftops.

I raised my gun and scanned the edges, but couldn't see anything.

"What do you have?"

But he was gone.

The grass where he was standing still waving in the wind.

I didn't see a body, couldn't hear a shot, but screamed.

"Down!"

I hit the dirt and began crab crawling forward, trying to zig, trying to zag, and hoping like Hell Bem and the Boy found cover.

Nothing happened.

I put a hundred yards between us, getting closer to the building, still hunting for what happened to Tyler, but there was no threat.

Nothing to see.

Nothing to hear.

Just the wind tickling the tops of the grass, whooshing over us.

My head rocked around to hunt for the kids, and sighed since they were hidden so well.

Both had scrambled into the weeds, both were stock still.

I could see a dull glint of sunshine on the Boy's rifle barrel but that was it.

From my vantage point I could see a store.

Glass whole, door shut, nothing moving.

We waited until I counted to three hundred, and then I moved.

"Check on Tyler."

I moved to my knees, aimed at the roof and watched.

The Boy crawled back to where Tyler was supposed to be but he wasn't.

"He's gone."

He must have seen something that spooked him and was flanking the town, or moving around to the opposite side.

I decided not to worry about him and focus on getting us to cover safely.

"Can you cover me?"

"I got you Dad," Bem sounded cold and clinical.

I hoppped up, stumbled and sprinted up to the storefront and under cover of the awning.

When I planted my back against brick, I waved her forward.

The Boy covered his sister while she sprinted to join me.

I popped out from the awning aiming up, which is as close to a direction as we could pinpoint potential problems.

Bem slapped into the brick, and the Boy was sprinting as soon as she hit the wall.

When they were beside each other and gasping, I ducked back under and planted next to him.

"Where's Tyler?" Bem worried.

"He can handle himself," I assured her.

"We need to find out what's out there."

"Why didn't they shoot?" the Boy wondered.

So did I.

Great question.

We were in the open, and exposed.

Anyone who felt threatened had a clean kill on any of us.

That's what I thought happened to Tyler, but no one was shooting.

Heck, no one was even threatening us.

It was just our guts screaming that something was wrong, someone was watching us.

I didn't feel like that under the awning.

:Did you see anything?"

The kids shook their heads, faces swiveling from one end of the street to the other.

:Still don't," said Bem.

"He's out there watching our backs," I told her.

I could see her shoulders visibly relax and almost growled.

But I'd figure that part out later.

I focused on the now.

Unknown threat.

Untouched store, or at least that's how it looked.

Empty town.

Lots of places for people to hide.

"Hi."

A tiny voice said from the corner of the building.

I whipped my gun around and watched a mop of blonde hair slip around the corner.

"Was that real?" the Boy sounded surprised.

"It wasn't a ghost," said Bem.

I scrambled up and gave chase.

A little boy stood his ground in the alley by the building, a wooden sword held in front of him, sharp point wavering.

He used his other hand to hold a smaller kid behind him.

The mop of blond hair.

I lowered my rifle.

"You're not going to hurt him," the older boy growled.

"Hi," said the blond.

Bem and the Boy rounded the corner behind me.

The tip of the sword bounced as he aimed at each of us.

"Are you alone?"

"Yes," said the little one.

"Shut up Rick," the big-eyed boy with the sword growled.

"Where are your parents?" Bem slid her rifle around to her back and went to one knee so she was on their level.

Rick, the tiny blond one sniffed as his lip trembled.

"You don't belong here," the older one pointed the sword.

It looked like it was made of balsa wood and would snap if he decided to stab her with it.

The layers of clothes she wore would protect her.

The two little boys wore practically nothing, just shorts and tank tops and mismatched shoes with the laces undone.

The outfits looked like they had been worn for a long time, dirt crusted layers almost crunching as they moved.

They were thin, almost emaciated.

Wild hair, wild eyes.

Feral.

"Do you belong here?" Bem soothed.

Tyler stepped around the back of the alley and stood as still as a statue while he watched.

"This is our town."

"We came in on the railroad," said Bem.

"Do you know where that is?"

"I didn't hear a train," said the older one.

"I'm Rick," the blond chimed in. "This is Carl."

"Hi Rick," Bem smiled. "Hi Carl. Are you guys hungry?"

The point of the sword wavered and dropped.

That was answer enough.

"We're going to go in the store and get some food.

Do you want to come with us?"

I locked eyes with Tyler and he made a slight shake with his head.

No one else out there.

We had found our watchers.

CHAPTER NINE

The two boys followed us into the store.

More precisely, they followed Bem into the store, keeping a wary eye on me and distance from the Boy and Tyler.

I can't say that I blame them.

I wasn't much to look at before the zombie Armageddon forever changed the population landscape of our country, and since then, I've been shot, blown up, stabbed, wrecked, tossed, and beaten on a weekly basis

It takes a toll on one's body and mine was no exception.

I had a long thick scar that gave my hair a new part just above my ear.

Scars around my eyes where people kept punching me, scrapes, cuts, bruises added to the ensemble.

Plus, I used to joke with my kids, I have a resting bitch face.

My normal look is pissed, even when I'm delighted.

They were always in a perpetual state of wonder growing up.

"What's wrong Dad?"

"Nothing. Why do you ask?"

"You look mad."

"I'm not mad, it's just my face.

"Not the best way to go through life, to constantly look concerned and on the verge of an anger management catastrophic breakdown, but such is luck.

I tried to mask it with jokes, and funny little songs.

Sometimes it worked.

But for little boys who just met an armed guy marching into town, I might have given me space and some sideways eye too.

The store was locked.

The Boy used a universal key to gain entry by busting out the glass in the door.

We stood back to do a Z check in case anything inside was drawn by the noise, but there was nothing.

"Where is everyone?" Bem asked the kids.

I didn't expect an answer, or at least one that made sense, but Carl surprised me.

"Gone."

His tiny voice was solemn.

"I'll show you," he offered.

She shot a raised eyebrow in my direction.

Should she go?

I slid my eyes from the Boy to Tyler and back again.

"Go with her," I told the scout. "Nothing happens to her. To them."

I tried not to make it sound menacing.

I really tried to rein in the threat in the tone.

But he shivered and nodded.

Quickly.

"Yes Sir."

Capital S.

"You're with me," I told the Boy before he could argue.

CHAPTER NINE

Bem made a noise in her throat, and I thought she was going to say she could take care of herself, but she held it in.

It made sense for her to have back up if we split up, and I did not like us splitting up.

If Tyler said the town was a population of two, then I was less worried.

A little less.

Not much.

I made sure the Boy and I hurried as we gathered supplies while Bem, Tyler and the two kids slipped back through the glass and onto Main street.

The inside of the store was pristine, if Spartan in choice.

There were about a dozen of every food item, and the choices were limited.

Mac n Cheese, Beans, Rice, Chili, Corn.

Still we were able to gather about a week's worth of meals, if we stretched it.

I was surprised there wasn't more, but it looked as if the clerk or owner had a big run on food, and just organized the remaining items before disappearing.

Or going Z.

"We'll check the houses too," I told the Boy.

He nodded and shouldered the heavier pack.

I smiled and took it from him.

"I got it," he tried to argue.

"I know you do."

But I took it from him and slid my arms through the straps.

Then I handed him a peanut candy bar that had been hidden behind the register.

"Save half for your sister."

His grin made me warm inside, and he smelled the wrapper,

vacuum sealed for freshness.

We made one more look around the store to see if we missed anything, and then made our way to the first house.

The front door was open.

The same with the kitchen cabinets.

"Rick and Carl?" said the Boy.

I nodded.

It was probably how to the two stayed alive.

We checked for weapons and kit in the bedrooms, but came up empty.

There was plenty there, but nothing compact we could carry back to the truck.

Most households are built to stay where they are, and travel time in the new zombie world was a minimalist paradise.

We still had a lot of daylight left and Kentucky was only a few hours away driving straight on the railroad.

"Leave it," I told him as he grabbed a comforter off the bed.

"We'll find something when we stop for the night."

He nodded, and we moved from house to house in silence.

The same story played out in each.

Open doors, empty pantries.

I'm glad the two little wild men had been able to stay alive, but it made for a light haul on our supply run.

We had found a couple of knives, and ammo for guns we didn't have by the time we reached the trailers and met up with Bem and Tyler.

That's when we found everyone else too.

CHAPTER TEN

"I see dead people," the Boy deadpanned.

The ground between the trailers was row after row of raised mounds, scrap board tombstones stuck haphazardly into the dirt.

I counted ten in the first row, and five rows deep.

"Did you do this?" Bem asked Carl and Rick.

The oldest pointed.

A rotting corpse leaned against a sign, legs splayed in an open grave.

The top of its head was missing.

"Was that your Dad?"

They both shook their moppet tops.

"Shane," said Rick." "He's dead."

That was a fitting epitaph for Shane I think.

"He was bit," Carl explained.

I held my breath and walked over.

A blood crusted pistol was between the skeletal legs of Shane.

He got bit and went out before he could go Z.

"How long ago?" I asked.

Trying to get a frame around how long they were alone.

The corpse looked like months.

"He did this," Rick offered.

"Is this the whole town Dad?"

I shrugged.

Bem sat on the ground and reached for the little one's hands.

Rick let her hold his, but Carl skittered away.

Who could blame him for trust issues.

"Let's check the trailers."

I pulled out a couple of pouches of food and handed it to Bem, then shot a look to Tyler to watch over her.

The Boy and I searched for more food.

We found where the boys had been sleeping.

It was trashed.

The food was gone though, hence the house scavenging or maybe Shane had done some stockpiling before he died.

There was none now though.

"Shane, you glorious bastard," I breathed when I opened the back bedroom door.

It had fifteen rifles, four pistols, ammo for all and a knife.

Whoever he had been, he was smart.

The guns had a long thin cable running through the trigger guards so the kids couldn't get them, and the ammo was at the top of the closet.

"I'll flip you for who gets to search the body for the key," I joked with my son.

He ran a hand across the top of the mirror on the dresser and showed me a tiny piece of metal, a victory smile plastered on his face.

"Kid's don't think to look high."

"You're a kid."

CHAPTER TEN

"Still am," he kept grinning and released the padlock.

I checked the action on a couple of hunting rifles, and matched ammunition to them.

We loaded them, and then did the same with pistols.

Back when gun control was a hot button issue, some proponents argued it was better to have it and not need it, than have the reverse be true.

I was indifferent at the time.

Growing up in the south meant guns were tools, no different than a hammer or screwdriver, just used for a purpose.

I wasn't in love with them, the way some folks were.

Since the Z though, better to have more than enough.

I adopted a SEAL philosophy I read somewhere.

Two is one, one is none and peace through superior firepower or something to that effect.

I handed a second rifle to the Boy, and a pistol.

He slung the first across his shoulder and seated the other in his waistband.

"Holsters might be good next time."

"Beggars and choosers," I told him.

"Just wishing out loud."

"We met the others back outside and I passed out weapons to Tyler and Bem.

She had Rick in her lap, and Carl was standing beside her, wiping pasta crumbs from his lips.

"They're coming with us," she told me.

Like I was going to leave two toddlers in the middle of a town.

It must be the face.

I tried on a smile, but the Boy shook his head.

"Give it up Dad," he grinned.

"Let's move out," I snorted.

37

Bem took her two new charges by the hand and led them toward the truck.

The little blond haired boy lasted longer than I thought he would before he asked to be carried.

She picked him up, and perched him on one hip as we went back to the railroad.

"I'm hungry," Carl said as Bem passed me the keys to unlock the truck.

I passed her my backpack of food as she settled in the backseat with the boys.

Tyler jumped in with them before I could object.

I don't know who growled louder, the Boy or me, but we let it pass as I gave him the keys.

"You drive," I told him and got a grin again.

He hopped behind the wheel, fired it up and we took off with a lurch that turned yells into giggles from the back.

11

CHAPTER ELEVEN

I was a notorious traffic hater before the plague.

I even adjusted my work hours just so I could avoid the most clogged and congested times of day.

There was no easier way to piss me off than to schedule something that put me in the cross hairs of traffic.

It was like building a bonfire at a gas station.

It might not blow up, but why take that chance?

Which is why I was in love with the railway car.

Truck.

The Boy locked in our speed at fifty miles an hour, slowing for curves and blind spots.

I liked his foresight.

He was being prepared in case we came up on something unexpected.

Tyler kept a rifle across his lap, ready, and Bem entertained the two little children in the back.

She teased their story out of them, or as close to one as she was going to get from their young minds.

Momma gone.

Dad never was.

Shane was a neighbor who helped.

Everyone died.

Shane killed a lot of them when they became monsters.

They couldn't play much anymore.

The older boy was seven and Momma left him to babysit his five year old brother.

A lot.

They broke into houses to eat, but always slept in Shane's trailer.

A sad story, but I bet it played out a lot across the country.

He said something I didn't understand, about a Wall, but couldn't explain it.

Told us Shane told him.

So we drove.

Bem hummed from the back seat as the younger boy leaned against her, the combination of the drive, the engine and a full bully lulling him to sleep.

"Bill Groggin's Goat?"

"What's that?" the Boy asked.

"A song. My Papaw used to sing it to us when we were kids."

"So it's ancient."

"Be nice."

"Come on Dad," the Boy grinned. "Did you and Papaw have to saddle up the horses to go look at the railroad when this happened.

"More like dinosaurs," Bem chimed in.

"I am Captain Caveman."

"Who?"

"Dear Lord up in heaven, please grant me the strength," I prayed and shook my head.

CHAPTER ELEVEN

My kids weren't raised around me as much as I would have liked, so I couldn't expose them to all the awesomeness that I remember from my childhood.

My brother and I would wake up on Saturday mornings and eat cereal in our tighty whities while we watched cartoons for a couple of hours.

Then mom would push us out of the door and lock the screen.

We were left up to our own devices until the streetlights came on.

There were ramps, and tree forts and bike roads across the city.

I think it said a lot about why I was so independent as an adult, and where I got a real "I'll figure it out" attitude that made me a decent jack of all trades.

But before the Z I wouldn't have let my kids roam around.

Too many crazies out there.

Kids got picked up off the side of the road when I was young, but the news didn't broadcast it twenty four seven.

And maybe because I had so many scars from childhood accidents, I didn't want to put my children through that.

I couldn't call these kids soft though.

Couldn't even think it, not after what they had been through, what they had done.

The Boy was a crack shot.

Tyler had been my number one scout for the group.

Bem had outwitted zombies and soldiers and survived lynch mobs and gangs.

Soft kids?

Like hell.

Chips off the old block.

Tiny polished diamonds, if you asked me.

Except they were woefully ignorant of car songs.

I blame myself.

When they were coming to visit me in Florida, and we had to drive, I would pick them up at seven or eight o'clock at night.

We would drive the two hours to Memphis, grab some food, and they could pass out while I drove through the darkness so they could wake up in Florida, or close enough.

After the sun came up and they were stirring, I was too zonked to think of car songs to sing.

The radio sufficed.

Hence my brain space dedicated to boy bands.

But no boy band had ever belted out Bill Groggin's goat with the level of passion I mustered as we drove along.

Not too loud though.

We were still surrounded by Z, even if we couldn't see them.

The iron wheels screeching on the rail was noisy enough that I imagined a herd of them vectoring our way.

CHAPTER TWELVE

'Dad. That is a shit ton of Zombies."

"Language," Bem said before I could.

Hey, it was the end of the world but that didn't mean we couldn't be polite.

He was one hundred percent correct though.

There were literally tons of zombies roaming inside the gate at Fort Knox.

The twelve foot perimeter fence was swarming with them, all circling in a mindless shuffle chasing whatever whim the wind carried along that distracted them.

They hadn't noticed us yet.

We came upon the complex but serendipity.

On the railroad tracks, we approached the countryside on the outskirts of Louisville and though we couldn't see the city yet, there were signs on the side of the track letting us know to slow down.

Or at least that's what it suggested to trains of old. As for us, we got wary. City meant more zombies, and also more bandits, marauders and other survivors who followed cavemen rules of survival. We happened across a sign that indicated a switch ahead that led to Fort Knox. "For the gold," the Boy said. I didn't know, so it sounded like a good working theory. We stopped to switch the tracks, use the trees for a potty break, then back in to get within a half mile of the fence.

The Army, in its infinite wisdom had cleared a mile's worth of trees between the forest and the base.

This made sense if they were ever to come under attack, though no one pointed out that a speeding train would make the distance in a few seconds, and if it was loaded with TNT or gun toting enemy, the open space would do little to stop them.

I was glad for the trees.

We held back in their shadows, and the zombies inside the fence couldn't see us.

If they did, the mass of them would knock it down as they began to herd after us.

The tiny boy beside Bem whimpered.

"We should go hide," his older brother whispered.

It sounded like good advice.

Keep moving, go find another base somewhere and get the map we needed.

Us versus a thousand walking dead was not good odds.

"Never tell me the odds," I muttered under my breath.

"What?" the Boy said out of the side of his mouth.

"I said we're going to fight the odds," and motioned them to follow me through the trees.

We worked around the perimeter of the fence line and it all looked whole.

CHAPTER TWELVE

And full of zombies.

Lots of rotting zombies.

Tyler caught a glint of sunlight off metal through the trees and motioned us to stop.

We watched him creep forward on the tips of his toes, barely making a sound as he moved, and when he stood up he waved us an all clear.

It was a road, two lane blacktop through a shallow gulch that led up to a guard shack with a closed gate.

Lined with civilian cars.

Several hundred of all makes and models lined both sides of the roads, bumper to bumper, stretching back almost a mile along the roadway.

"Oh, that's why," said the Boy.

He pointed to a sign next to the guard shack.

It was black paint stenciled on plywood, and looked like whoever made it had been in a hurry.

Drips of paint dried down the board, looking like a leaking wound.

REFUGEE CENTER

No wonder the Fort was so full.

"Bis was in a place like this?" the Boy breathed out a sigh.

I held mine in.

My little girl had been in something like this, if they made it.

Even now, she might be a Z, one of the walking dead roaming the countryside, gone from me.

Hunting for her was pointless.

The US had a population of four hundred million people and who knows how many were dead, how many were Z and how many were survivors.

Finding her would be impossible, especially if this place was like every other refugee center in America.

"We'll find her," my voice was steady.

I let the rage bubble up a little in my gut, let it fuel the fire and felt it harden my resolve.

We would.

Never tell me the odds.

"I have an idea," Tyler shouldered his rifle.

He looked up one long line of cars and down the other.

"Anyone bring marshmallows?"

CHAPTER THIRTEEN

His plan was a good one.

I wish I'd thought of it.

I sent him and the Boy to escort Bem back to the rail truck with the two children so they would be safe.

"Lock it up," I instructed her. "Keep your rifle ready."

She almost rolled her eyes then stopped herself and I smiled.

"Sorry kid, it's tough to switch out of Dad mode. I know you've made it this far."

"Not just my looks," she said.

Reminding me she was a thinker.

Strategic.

I'd seen her in an arena full of zombies, put there by a man who hated me.

She gutted one, smeared its insides on her clothes and sat still while the others ignored her.

Sharp.

I wished I was more like her.

The five of them walked back through the woods, and I listened.

Trying to hear other threats, head cocked to one side to gauge the bird song, the insect hum, any change in volume or tempo that would indicate a threat.

Then I pulled a knife from it's sheath and got to work.

I punched holes in the gas tanks, and let the gasoline leak out of the cars onto the blacktop.

I was through twenty cars on one side when my son and Tyler came back.

"They're safe," the Boy said.

They pulled knives and we made short work of the rest of the vehicles.

After twenty minutes, we had a long line of cars that made a metal tunnel all the way to the gate, except for the last thirty feet, which the guards had kept clear.

Our movement in the roadway attracted some Z, who pressed against the gate, bending it out and bowing it forward.

More Z were drawn by the others, and the weight began to stress the metal with creaks and clangs that could be heard over the moans and grunts of the zombies.

"Not much time," Tyler commented.

I studied our work.

"Good enough for government," I said and ushered the two boys back to the end of the line of cars.

"Hey," I called after Tyler. "Lighter."

He felt in his pockets and shrugged.

"Left mine at the last campsite."

The Boy shook his head.

"I don't have one either."

"Damn it."

A great plan we were about to toss because we couldn't light a fire.

CHAPTER THIRTEEN

"Check the cars!"

I hauled open a door and sniffed, to see if I could smell the stale stench of a smoking habit, but couldn't make out the scent of anything over the gas that puddled at our feet.

It was a hand to hand search, ripping through consoles, and dashboards, quick glances at the floorboards.

I was in car number five when the gate broke.

"Back," I screamed and waved my arms so the Z would still funnel into the tunnel.

I could hear the boys running behind me, then the sound of car doors opening and slamming as they continued the search.

I had to hop and walk backwards, keeping the Z focused on me so they wouldn't spread out into the woods.

"Found one!" the Boy shouted.

I turned and ran to him, taking the lighter from his hands, then Tyler joined us and we jogged to the end of the rows.

We waited.

The Z were coming, a tide of shambling corpses grunting, and lurching toward us.

We wouldn't get them all, but several hundred piled into the tunnel, a herd size drawn by the movement through the gate, drawn by each other.

"Now," said Tyler.

"Not yet."

They drew closer.

Twenty yards.

Ten.

"Now!" said the Boy.

"Everyone is a critic," I flicked the wheel on the lighter as I kneeled down to the gas puddle on the blacktop.

It sparked, but no fire.

"Dad!"

Tyler raised his rifle and shot the first Z as it lunged for my head.

I fell backwards, crab walking as more zombies came at us.

I could only use my feet and one hand, the other thumb scratching the lighter, trying to get a flame.

The Boy added his shots to Tyler's and kept the front row of grasping hands off me.

We worked our way backwards, and the gas puddle ended.

I spun the wheel one more time and it sparked.

Flames licked up across the back of my hand and raced in a blue orange conflagration under the Z, the fire making a roaring sound as it ignited the black top.

I jumped up and danced back, shaking my hand.

The Boy sent a bullet into the head of two Z that lumbered out of the fire.

Tyler picked off the ones on the front line.

I pulled my pistol, ignoring the searing burn on the back of my hand as I added my shots to theirs.

We knocked down the front line, then the second, which created a tiny burning barrier of zombies that held the others back.

The flames burned through the legs, knocking more down, and dry clothes caught fire until the air was full of bar b que zombie, a cloying stench that rolled out of the tunnel of cars in a toxic fog.

Then one of the vehicles popped and exploded.

I thought we would be okay since we released the gas vapors from the tank, which is why most cars explode.

It's not like it was in the movies, a violent flipping of the automobile with lots of pyrotechnics.

CHAPTER THIRTEEN

Just a loud whoosh and pop, followed by more black smoke that filled the space between the tress, and blocked our view of the rest of the Z at the gate.

The flames would draw even more.

Exploding cars compounded our danger, especially since we couldn't predict when they would go.

"Back to the truck," I ordered and we took off through the trees.

CHAPTER FOURTEEN

The truck was empty.

I pulled up short at the tree line and glared up and down the track.

"Is she ducking down?" the Boy whispered next to me.

Tyler ducked into the trees and moved further away from us.

He studied the tracks, studied the truck.

I motioned the Boy down and behind a pine.

"Bem!" I called out hoping she would lift her head.

But she didn't.

"Watch."

I moved out of the pines and ran up to the side of the truck, ducked down against it.

I reached over and knocked on the door with three quick slaps.

No answer.

I peeked into the windows, into the truck bed.

Empty.

Tyler stepped out of the trees and gave a low whistle.

The Boy joined me as we jogged a couple hundred feet up the tracks.

CHAPTER FOURTEEN

"Struggle," he said and pointed to scuff marks on the ground.

We followed it along the railroad tracks, spread out.

I kept the Boy close to the forest, and angled away from Tyler in an attempt to minimize our target signatures.

The trail led us to a path in the woods.

"Scuffle," said Tyler.

He bent down on one knee and studied the ground.

The leaves were messed up in front of the truck door, the supplies missing.

"They went that way," the Boy added.

Not to be outdone.

I checked the safety on my rifle.

"Stay close," I growled.

There were patches of pine needles and leaves overturned leading into the woods.

Bem was dragging a foot, brushing against tree bark to scrape off one side.

Smart girl.

Making it easy to follow.

The trail converged with others.

"How many?"

Tyler shrugged.

"A lot," said the Boy.

A dozen different sets of boot prints.

They took my girl.

They could have been watching us now.

"Stop," I whispered.

We stood there like statues and I wanted to blend into the ground, the trees, anything we could hide behind.

I couldn't tell you what set it off.

It wasn't the crack of a branch, or some other noise that stood out on the path in the forest.

It may have been the smell, the reek of unwashed bodies and hand rolled cigarettes carried on the wind.

I could smell it now, faintly on the breeze.

Someone had been smoking in an enclosed environment and the stench of it clung to them like body odor.

"Dad?" the Boy whispered.

I turned my head and he flicked his eyeballs in a direction off to the right.

The trees were moving.

No, it wasn't the trees, it was men and women dressed in camo detaching themselves from the tress.

It was a good pattern, good blend because standing under the shadows of the oaks and evergreens, they mixed in with the bark.

That's what it was then.

Movement that didn't match mother nature.

My eyes recognized it before my brain could figure it out.

Score one for natural instincts.

Not that it did us any good.

We were still surrounded as the group of nine stepped out of the forest on the path in front of and behind us.

They were on both sides too.

Nine of them, muffled in thick all weather gear, heads wrapped in hoods and scarves and thick thermals that made them appear to be puffy large human shaped monsters.

There was a piece of good news though.

Only one carried a gun.

Bem's gun.

The figure stepped out of the circle and closer to me.

"Are you the leader of this here outfit?"

CHAPTER FOURTEEN

It was a woman by her voice, but I could tell nothing else.

Even her height was disguised by thick hiking boots that must have added another couple of inches and the hood over a beanie on her head.

"Where is she?"

The woman pointed my daughter's gun in my direction.

"I asked you a question," she growled back. "It's rude not to answer."

Leave it to the South to insist on the social niceties even after a zombie apocalypse has devastated the world.

"Sorry," I grumbled. "Where is she, please?"

That earned a chuckle from a couple of the men, which seemed to piss her off.

I wasn't worried about getting shot.

I've been shot and it hurts like Hell, not an experience I want to go through again.

The only reason I wasn't worried is because the woman wore thick gloves and her fingers couldn't fit through the trigger guard, at least not while they were on.

"Get the boys," she said.

The men on both sides of us jumped on the Boy and Tyler, yanking them away from the circle of the rest of them who closed in tighter around me.

I wished we were in a kung fu movie.

It was always funny to me how Jackie Chan or Bruce Lee could take on twenty men at a time, but they all fought one by one.

A giant circle of warriors would surround the hero but then totally give up their advantage by only taking him on in tiny little individual attacks.

The filmmakers tried to make it look more dangerous by letting the hero block one guy, or avoid another even as a second attacked, but it just wasn't realistic.

I'm not what you could expect from the movies about being realistic though.

In real life, a group of six guys surround you, they don't fight one by one.

They rush in and tackle you to the ground, kick, stomp, punch, grunt.

I'm lucky they didn't bite.

Two of them held my arms, two held my legs and the other two practiced their tap dance lessons on my rib cage, stomach and thighs.

When one decided to play field goal kicker with my head, I didn't want to play anymore and passed out.

CHAPTER FIFTEEN

I woke up alone in the middle of a field.

That wasn't quite right, I thought. I had to shake my head a couple of times to clear the cobwebs.

One of my eyes was crusted shut with something.

Blood.

I reached up to try and wipe it away, but my hands were tied behind my back.

The field was an amphitheater of some sort. I glanced left and right, but the kids weren't with me.

I tried to turn around and rough hands grabbed me, jerked me back forward to face the stage.

A large woman sat on a throne in the middle. She stared down at me with eyes that drilled into me.

I felt like a bug under a microscope the way she studied, her lips pressed together in a half snarl.

She had long red hair, bright eyes and wore hunters overalls like the rest of her men. It was a little warm for the extra layers, but smart. The bibs were thick padding and good armor against a zombie.

I made a note to scrounge up a pair for us and looked down at myself.

I could see why she thought I was a bug.

My clothes were ripped and tattered from the fight in the woods. Smoke and soot covered what I could see of my skin peeking through the tears. I'm sure it covered my face and what was left of my hair too.

Scorched, beaten and bloody.

That had to be what she saw.

"You got a name?" she asked.

"The one my mother gave me," I shot back.

She grinned and snickered.

"I'm Mags," she said. "You think you're a tough guy, don't you? I've known a lot of tough guys in my day."

She lifted a leg and draped it over the side of the chair.

There was too much room between us for me to make a lunge for her, too many unknowns at my back.

And the guys lining the stage behind her were a big reason to hold still too. A dozen or so of them, all armed with rifles, all glaring at me.

I bet they could take me down before I made it ten steps. Maybe five.

"You like my Colonels?" she asked. "They're a Kentucky tradition."

"That's a lot of chiefs," I croaked.

She smiled and nodded.

Someone grabbed my arms and lifted me up, straining my shoulder against the tight bindings strapping the wrists together.

They spun me around.

Mags was at my back. She moved to the edge of the stage and

CHAPTER FIFTEEN

said in a soft voice.

"Lots of Indians."

The amphitheater behind me was full of people. Stands on either side packed ground to top with armed men. Some soldiers, some hunters, but all of them watching me with intense interested stares.

"Did I just hear you gulp?" Mags giggled.

"Just wondering how many I have to kill to get out of here."

The hands spun me around again, rougher this time and knocked me to the mud. They lifted me just as rough and held straight.

"There's a difference between tough and just plain dumb," Mags crinkled her nose.

I huffed out a breath and sniffed.

"You've got to want something," I said. "Otherwise I'd be dead. Unless you're one of those evil Bond villains who likes to spill their guts about world domination while I

hatch an escape plot?"

Mags clapped her hands together.

"I do think you are a delight," she drawled. "My boys said you put up a good fight out in our woods. And you're right, if I wanted you dead, you would be a doornail."

She winked at one of the men behind me and he sliced through the plastic at my wrist. Two zip ties dropped onto the ground at my feet.

"Now I'm not saying you won't be dead once we're done," she cackled. "But at least you can say I gave you a fighting chance as a thank you for clearing those zombies out of the Refugee Center at the Fort. That gave us a lot of supplies. I'm grateful."

"Thankful enough to just let me go?"

The cackle again and this time another motion.

"I'm the head of the Council in here. That makes me the boss. And as the boss, everyone in here does exactly what I say. Sometimes without me even asking."

I heard someone moving in on me and ducked as a fist slid over my head. I kicked out with my foot and cracked the inside of the man's knee.

It folded out with a loud snap and he screamed as he fell.

Mags darted back as more men rushed in.

"There's only two ways this can end sister."

She glared at me.

I wasn't trying to be misogynistic by calling her sister, I was trying to goad her into acting from anger.

People do dumb things when they're angry.Like trek half way across the country to rescue kids who were probably dead, and then reversing direction to do it again.

The odds were almost always against doing dumb things.

Except God or whatever passed for it in this new zombie plagued world had a soft spot for dumb guys and their children.

I wished it were for all children but I'd seen some kid Z and it broke my heart.

"You will comply," she said in a crisp voice.

"We are Borg, huh? Resistance is futile."

She made a small motion with her left hand and the gate on stage left popped open.

A bunch of rough looking guys started marching through.

Six of them, so maybe it wasn't that many, but six on one never looked pretty.

She was too far away to see me gulp.

I tried to think of that line from Princess Bride where the dread pirate fights the giant, and he can't think of how to beat him because he's used to fighting groups of men, but it escaped me.

CHAPTER FIFTEEN

Leave it to the zombie apocalypse to cut into quality movie memorization time.

I settled for an old comic book stand by."

Bring it on."

Or maybe it was a cheerleading movie, but in the middle of the beginning of a fight, no one bothers to check on your references.

They rushed all at once, proving they didn't watch kung fu movies.

Those guys would wait patiently while you smacked their buddy around, then come in when it was there turn.

These guys didn't get the memo.

Just for perspective, there are at least six ways to reach a body when you bum rush it.

Front, back, side one, side two, top and bottom.

These fellas were going to grab my arms, one to each, torso and neck, and I wasn't really sure what the other two planned.When the first two made their move and clamped on my wrists, I dropped.I wish I could say it was skill and planning on my part, but remember that whole God loves dumb asses theme I'm building? I really just slipped trying to back up, and the two holding me by the wrist were slammed forehead to forehead when they refused to let go of my arms.Bonk.The torso guy launched himself at the same time I fell, so he overshot me and gave me a good goose egg with his boot as he sailed over me.Number four was dry humping my leg as I went down.At least that's what it felt like.I let him have his fun, since number five towered over me and drew back his boot for a kick.

I used my now freed hand to punch him in the nuts, and squeezed for all I was worth.

I got a chest full of vomit for my trouble, but he was out of the picture.

Dry humper must have finished, but instead of rolling over and falling asleep, he tried to claw his way up to my face.

I grabbed him by the back of the hair and rubbed his nose in my freshly decorated chest.

For the record, if someone rubs your face in another guy's throw up, you will probably throw up yourself.

It was warm and chunky and had I eaten recently, I would have added my own repast to the two recent meals residing on my person.

Urgh.

Number six kicked me in the thigh vacated by the dry humper, and it hurt.

I was going to feel that tomorrow.

If I was going to make it to tomorrow, I needed to turn the tide, and not in a return the vomit comet kind of way.

Rule number which one, I forget, but it's don't be on your back in a fight.

So I started rolling, trying to bowl out some legs, trying to get clear of the group of them. I gained space and pushed up just in time to see a steel toe aimed at my eyeball.

I ducked away and managed to take a scraping blow across my healing bullet scar, and hopped, skipped and jumped backwards more as stars exploded around my vision.

There were now eight of them standing in front of me, but when I shook my head, some of the twins disappeared, and left four standing.

One of the guys holding my wrist was knocked cold by his noggin bump with his buddy, the guy next to him was still clutching his crotch.

Guess I must have popped something.

The rest didn't rush this time.

They spread out in a wider pattern, eyes bouncing off me to each other and back again as they tried to decide what to do next.

"Get him," Mags screamed an order.

I guess she expected them to make short work of me, or that I would go quietly.

She was right about one thing.

I was going to be very quiet.

The four men screamed and rushed again.

I ran to meet them halfway. Of course, we're only talking ten steps or so for the distance between us, but since they were screaming, they were losing air.

I dropped to my knees and slid into one, punching for gut with the sharp point of my elbow, straight into his diaphragm.

The combo sent him sprawling, stomach heaving as he gasped for wind.

Going low threw the one beside him off.

He rounded on me with a haymaker, but I spun and did my best sweep the leg move into both of his ankles.

One snapped and he screamed. I kept spinning, tossing up little clouds of dirt and debris when the other two guys landed on top of me.

They were good at punching.

Experts even.

One was hammering on the top of my head with one fist, clenching my shirt with the other as I kept my chin pressed against his neck.

The other was trying to compose a drum symphony on my kidneys.

A long one.

But that left my hands free.

I was fighting blind and just reaching, but hooked a finger in someone's mouth on one hand, a thumb in the other's eye and pulled with both.

I got a reward.

An eyeball popped on my thumb and sent warm juice running down my arm, and I felt what it was like to have a cheek rip open on my hand, then a warm spurt of blood cascading down that arm.

Those guys screamed, or maybe it was me.

When they rolled away in the dirt, I added some of my own vomit to the gunk already on my chest, even though I hadn't eaten.

Then I stood up and faced the woman in the chair. I wanted to say something smart ass, or snarky, but close quarter fighting leaves one breathless.

Plus, my side hurt.

I bet I would piss some blood that night.

If I made it that far.

Six bodies lay on the ground around me, none of them dead, but all of them squirming.

It really looked like something I would like to do, but I felt I had an image to maintain.

The whole predators don't show weakness to other predator's thing.

"Impressive," she said in her flat voice.

I was glad the collective approved, and wondered why they didn't just shoot.

They had guns.

Was this some sort of test?

Did I pass?

"Can I just take my kid and go?"

She smiled then, and I did not like the way she wore it on her face.

A shark's smile under bored impassive eyes, or like a cat toying with its lunch.

"Kid?" she asked with pretended innocence. "Or kids?"

Another flick of her finger brought Tyler and the Boy to the stage, joined by Bem.

My stomach did a flip flop thing, but on a bright note, it totally made me forget about the mish mash of my kidneys.

"Bring out the giant," she said.

CHAPTER SIXTEEN

And then the giant showed up. It's not often you get the chance to say that in real life.

I wouldn't have suspected an NFL player to survive the zombie plague, but for the life of me I couldn't fathom why I thought that. Of course some would survive.

They are extraordinary athletes, and with a couple of thousands of them, it would only make sense.

This guy looked like a sumo wrestler met a mack truck and they made a baby.

A big giant bald headed baby glaring at me with pig eyes and what I hoped was oil that made his muscles shine.

"You're dead," he predicted.

I almost nodded.

He was probably right.

I'm not a large man, and trekking half way across the country scavenging for food made me wiry.

All muscle, sure, but there wasn't much of it, as far as raw brute strength.

The giant on the other hand looked well fed.

Like he ate whole turkeys every day.

And washed them down with protein shakes.

Size isn't everything.

At least that's what we tell the ladies.

Big meant he was going to be slow.

Which I was not.Big meant he would have more weight to carry and tire easy.

I was fast on my feet and a long distance runner to boot.

My mind raced.

It was going to be an Ali Frazier fight, the old Rope a Dope.

I'd wear him out by staying out of reach, and when he got tired, move in and finish him, just like the man suggested to Johnny at the all karate valley championship.

Then he moved.Like a dancer, fast and lithe and his dad must have really been a Mack truck because he was going as fast as one.I barely had a chance to dodge out of his grip and then it was on.

He was too big, too fast and looked too strong.

I was too tired, too beat and too broken to win.

This wasn't going to be fair at all.

I kept backing up, all the while thinking of Ali and Foreman. Rope a dope would work great on this massive stack of humanity, but I wasn't sure I could handle a hit.

Then he did.

And I couldn't.

It was a glancing blow across the scarred side of my head and sent me reeling.

Then his speed kicked in and he landed one on my chin.

It would have been better it knocked me cold.

But all it did was hurt.

And bleed.

He grabbed me in a bear hug and squeezed. Ribs cracked.

My arms were pinned but my hands were free. I grabbed for his nuts and squeezed.

He giggled in my face and laughed.

"Ain't that kind of date," his breath smelled like coffee.

He planted his forehead into my nose, once, twice and stars exploded in my head.

Then he dropped me, straddled my chest and started pounding with massive ham sized fists.

I saw two, a third, then no more.

CHAPTER SEVENTEEN

I woke up some time later and stared at the white walls around me.

Plain, unadorned and unbroken except for a door and a window that looked out onto a courtyard, a sliver of blue sky visible at the top of the building across the way.

My throat was sandpaper.

I tried to move my hands, but soft cushioned cuffs held them strapped to a bar on the side of the bed.

The door open and a tall white haired orderly in blue scrubs peeked in.

"You're awake," he smiled.

His face was kind, soft, thin hair touching the back of his scrub collar.

He stepped into the room.

"I'm Tony," he said. "You've been out for a while. Are you thirsty?"

I tried to answer, but it came out as a croak that cracked and evolved into coughing fit.

He put a hand on my chest and nursed me through it, then held a small pink plastic cup full of water up and put a straw to my lips.

"Just a sip," he ordered. "You've been in and out for days."

I took two long swallows, almost crying at how good it felt as the moisture coated my mouth and throat.

The sandpaper melted into something like gravel and I tried again.

"Where are my kids?"

Tony smiled and nodded.

He must have been a priest before or some social worker. There was an air of kindness about him, a patience.

"You've mentioned them before," he answered. "The doctor is on his way and he'll be able to answer more questions."

Tony checked the straps on my wrists, double checked the ones on my ankles and gave me another sip of water.

"You said days," I told him. "How many?"

"You've been in here for almost a month."

My stomach dropped.

A month.

What had Bem and the Boy done? What were they doing to them? Bis out there, somewhere for a month on her own.

I struggled against the bindings.

Tony put his hand on my chest again.

"Hold on," he said. "Let's just relax."

"I've got to get out of here."

"That's what you said before we put you under last time."

"Put me under?"

The door opened and a woman stepped inside. She had brown hair, large eyes and a serious look on your face.

She marched across the room and took a chart off the end of the hospital bed.

"You had us worried," she studied the chart. "We weren't sure you were coming back this time."

"This time? Who are you?"

She peered over the end of the clipboard and watched me, pen poised on the chart.

"You really don't remember me?"

I shook my head.

She made a note on the paper.

"I've been your doctor for the last six months. You're in a hospital."

I tried to gesture to the white walls, but the sarcasm was lost on her.

"I can see. The giant must have done a number on me."

"What giant?" she asked as she scribbled another note.

I looked from her to the orderly and back again.

"Your giant, the one the lady turned loose."

"What lady?"

I screwed up my eyebrows.

She told me her name. I tried to recall it. Marge. Maggie.

"Mags," I stuttered.

The doctor stared at Tony for a moment then back at me. She had a sad look in her eyes.

"There's no one named Mags here."

I struggled to sit up again, and Tony held be against the bed. It wasn't difficult for him to do.

"Where are my kids?!"

"You need to relax, please," said the doctor. "I don't want to sedate you again."

I fought for control and laid down. I didn't want them to sedate me. I needed answers.

"I told him he's been asking for his kids," said the orderly.

"Do you know where you are?"

I shook my head.

"Some compound. Kentucky."

It was her turn to shake her head.

"You are in Kentucky," she spoke in a slow controlled manner. "But you're not in a compound. This is a hospital. A psychiatric facility. You have had a break with reality and have been our guest for the past nine months."

Break with reality? Nine months?

But all I could manage was, "Huh?"

"I've had you under constant monitoring. You just came off a seventy two hour suicide watch. I kept you sedated so you wouldn't hurt yourself."

The door opened and a thick necked black man leaned in.

"Doc, we need you. It's an emergency."

She hung the chart on the foot of the bed and patted my shin.

"I'll come back and see you in a little while. I need you to relax. Stay calm and we'll get you some answers."

I watched her leave.

The black man smiled at me.

"I'm glad you're coming around."

"Do I know you?"

The smile fell.

"It's Jeffrey, man. You've known me since you've been here."

"I have?"

"Yeah, you and I are good friends. At least when you're like this. The other way," he shuddered and shared a glance with Tony.

"What other way?"

CHAPTER SEVENTEEN

Tony waved him out of the room.

"We're not going to get you excited. Just try to get some rest and I'll be back after rounds."

Tony ushered Jeffrey out of the room and left me alone strapped to the bed with nothing but my jumbled and confused thoughts.

Nine months?

CHAPTER EIGHTEEN

Three days.

I was strapped to the bed for three days. I counted the passage of time as the sun slanted through the window and climbed across the wall.

Tony or Jeffrey would come and feed me, pudding or soup, but they wouldn't loosen the straps and they wouldn't talk.

They would come back later with a bedpan.

The doctor checked in twice a day, but she wouldn't say anything either.

It's like they were afraid to tell me anything.

Finally, Jeffrey said it was time to go for a walk.

He unstrapped my feet first.

Tony stood by the door while he unfastened my left wrist, then my right. Jeffrey stepped back fast and waited.

I struggled to sit up, but I was weak.

Soup, pudding and atrophy.

It took two tries to swing my legs off the bed, and three tries to stand up. I wobbled and held fast to the end of the bed.

"Short walks," Tony said and stepped into the corridor.

I took a step after him, almost falling, but caught myself.

Then another, balance coming back.

The tile floor was cold under my bare feet.

Jeffery came up and put his hand on my elbow, guiding me, but not too hard, not too fast.

"Small steps," he said.

We took small steps through the door and out into the hall.

There were other rooms off of this one, doors closed and hiding occupants.

The white walls were pristine, looking almost new.

The tile was shining, and sunlight beamed through double doors at the end of the corridor.

Tony stood by an empty nurse's station and watched Jeffrey lead me down the hall.

"To the bathroom and back," he advised.

Jeffrey nodded and steered me toward a doorway.

My legs were shaking from lack of use.

It was tough to catch my breath.

We made the bathroom doorway and Jeffrey led us inside.

Yellow square tiles covered the walls up to head height, two stalls and two sinks under a long mirror.

"I have to warn you," said Jeffrey. "You did some awful things to yourself while you were in a delusional state."

"What kinds of things."

He pointed to the mirror and I saw myself for the first time in weeks.

Maybe even months.

Long hair with gray streaks, stubble, dark sunken eyes in a

hollowed-out face.

Pale.

Not the tan smiling face I was used to seeing from Florida.

And scars.

A long one that ran over the side of my head drawing a thick white line that was crudely stitched with white x scar tissue.

More scars, tiny purple and red lines across the side of a face that looked older than I remembered, more worn.

And then I locked on my eyes.

I'm not sure if anyone has ever stared in a mirror and tried to see their own soul.

That type of look is usually reserved for lovers, because we live with so many lies that we tell ourselves we can't handle that level of truth.

The eyes didn't lie.Brown pupils with flecks of gold, crinkled memories of laugh lines etched in the skin around them.

They stared back at me and I remembered.

I remembered being blown up by a grenade tossed in a tunnel, protecting a young boy who tried to build a kingdom.

Byron.I remembered being nursed back to health more than once by a woman a decade or more my junior that I rescued from a cult.

A woman who loved me, and who I may have been falling in love with back.

Anna.

And Brian.

My friend who wanted my counsel, who wanted to lead a group and keep them safe, who believed in society and rebuilding something better from the ground up.

Were they all figments of my creation?My imagination?

Were my children safe in Arkansas and Florida, doing teenage things like texting and chatting, homework and crushing on boys, girls, and thinking how their parents didn't really know how the world worked?Were they okay?

The Mississippi River.

The flight.

My son the pilot.

The fighting.

The gunshots.

And what felt like a thousand zombies.

Did I fall into a coma or stupor and imagine it all?

"No," I said.

"It's true," said Jeff.

He put a gentle hand on my shoulder and steered me toward the door."

"The mind is an incredible and powerful thing. You have convinced yourself of many things. And you have hurt people. That's why we sedated you."

I let him lead me back to the room.

My brain was tumbling like a boulder down a mountain, an avalanche of emotion that threatened to crush me, drag me under and I felt like I was suffocating.

"How long?" I croaked and cleared my throat.

"Your chart says a couple of years. We've only seen you for nine months."

The purple scar on my head could be that old.

And self-mutilation would be on my face, my hands, arms and legs where I could see.

Where I could reach.

But I couldn't feel his hand on my back.

Or part of his hand, really.

The other part was dead.

Like I had a strip of skin that no longer felt anything but pressure.

I concentrated on his touch.

Fingers, yes.

Tips pressing against flesh.

One. Two.

Almost three. Thumb.

First finger.

Where were the rest?

Pressure, sure, but it felt different.

I needed to see.

I shifted and turned around.

"Where are you going?"

Did he sound worried?

I saw his finger flick and one of the orderlies shift away from the nurse's station.

I glanced down at my hand.

There was a burn scar on the back of it, healing but no longer red.

From a fire trap set for zombies.

I didn't answer him as I edged back into the bathroom and fumbled the ties of the hospital gown.

It slid off my neck and dropped on the floor in a puddle at my feet.

More scars on my chest, a pucker wound.

That didn't look self inflicted.

I shifted sideways.

Whip scars, red, raised whelps and lines slowly healing.

Purple mass of bruises turning green, blue and yellow.

And burn scars like tiger stripes.

I couldn't make them all out, they curled around out of my

site.

I twisted further just to see how far I could see.

Jeff stood in the door, the orderly at his back.

He watched me twist, then smirked when I made eye contact. "Be kind of hard to do those yourself, huh cowboy?"

He reached into the pocket of the white coat and pulled out a plastic tipped syringe.

He used his thumb to flip the cap off. It clattered to the floor in front of them.

"Hold him."

Tony surged past him and took three steps forward. In the spirit of my ancestors, the Scots have fought in kilts for centuries.

That meant an army of free balling warriors running into battle.

Before that, the Picts who settled Ireland would fight in the nude.

It unnerved the enemy.

I called upon the ghosts of my warriors, let the orderly take one more step, then tried to kick him in the chin.

By way of his groin.

It wasn't much of a fight.

It felt like squashing two small oranges in a sack.

It sounded like it too.

The man sucked in wind and collapsed.

It couldn't even be called the fetal position because babies can't curl up that tight.

Guess he was free balling too under his white scrubs.

Jeffrey backed out of the bathroom, and tried to grab the door.

I hit it with my shoulder, slammed it out of his hand.

He dropped the needle and pounded up the hallway.

I spent a half second deciding if I should pick it up, made a scoop for it and missed.

Then my feet slapped on the linoleum after him before he could reach another door and lock me in.

It was tough.

I was weak.

My muscles weren't moving like I wanted them to, like I asked them to do.

My mind was in a fog, but it was burning away in a heat of rage that boiled up out of my gut.

Drugs, I thought.

They drugged me.

The rage shot adrenaline through my system, and even though I was wobbly, like a foal in spring time, I felt better.

No, I felt mad.

Madder.

I lurched and shambled after Jeffrey.

If he got help, it was going to be a lot harder to get out of here.

CHAPTER NINETEEN

I followed Jeffrey through the door and pulled up short.

Mags was waiting for me on the sidewalk, a half dozen Colonel's at her back. They were armed, but so far nothing was pointed in my direction.

"Speak of the devil," she drawled. "And look who shows up."

Part of me wanted to cover up, but I'd left the hospital gown in the bathroom. I had no choice but to stand there flapping in the wind.

"They boy might have been running cause a naked man was chasing him," Mags laughed. "But if you wanted to chase me some I might get caught."

She winked.

There must have been some motion in it, something I didn't see because the Colonel's fanned out to either side of me.

Still no guns, but hands ready.

"You want to walk with me?"

"I don't have a thing to wear."

That made her laugh, but it was a mad sort of giggle, like Mags had lost her mind in the Kentucky bluegrass.

"Would you feel better in pants?"

"I'd feel dressed for bear with one of those rifles."

She slapped a hand on her hip and giggled again.

"You must be trying out to be my next husband, because nothing is sexier than a naked man holding a gun, I swear."

But she didn't give me one.

Instead she nodded to one of the men on my right.

He took two steps in, pulled an emergency blanket out of his coveralls and tossed it to me.

I took my time unfolding the mylar blanket, and instead of draping it around my shoulders, wrapped it around my waist like a towel.

Or kilt.

A silver space age kilt.

Mags nodded in approval.

"Ready?"

"As I'll ever be."

I fell in step with her, though there was distance between us. The Colonel's packed in tight, this time rifles held ready in case I did something stupid I suppose.

I thought it was a bit of overkill, you know, drugged up guy wobbling along in a shining shimmery piece of plastic, but I guess they knew something about me.

"Where are my children?"

"They're safe," she said. "For now."

Rage gurgled at the threat.

But I held it in check.

"I wonder what you were like before?" Mags pondered.

CHAPTER NINETEEN

It seemed like a rhetorical question so I kept quiet.

"I was a Mom first, then I started my own business. I made wine in a vineyard a couple hundred miles from here. Can you believe that?"

I nodded.

I had no idea what a winemaker looked like, so her being one was as good as gold for me.

"Got any bottles left?"

"Sure," she grinned and watched me from the corner of her eyes. "Got a whole basement full of them. After this is all over, you drop by for a bottle and I'll give you your pick."

"When what is all over?"

She led me from the courtyard between two wings of the building they called a hospital.

"This. The zombies."

"You think it's going to be over?"

"Sure I do. We all do. I'm on the Council here, and we're waiting for the High Council to rescue us."

I wasn't sure what she was talking about.

I'd been from Florida to Arkansas and back, and hadn't seen any sign of authority other than what little potentates were declaring themselves.

I just assumed this compound was another one, and her wide eyes and temperament convinced me I wasn't wrong.

Until now.

"I've been on my own for awhile," I told her. "I haven't been keeping up with the news."

"No man is an island." That's what she said.

Like she was reading it from a philosophy book or something.

Her hazel eyes drilled into mine as she pretended to plumb my depths.

"We're waiting here," she said. "The Council has a role to keep our citizens safe until order can be restored."

"That's good," I told her.

I wanted her on my side.

"But you're a threat to our peace."

"I'm not the one who kidnapped a little girl."

"Rescued a teenager from a dangerous man."

"I'm her father."

"Genetics don't make you any less dangerous," she corrected me.

I bit my tongue.

It was tough.

"You had her in some ill conceived plan to kill the walking dead and you set our forest on fire."

Spittle flew off her lips as she pivoted and glared at me.

"Do you have any idea what you've done?"

Killed a couple thousand Z.

Moved a threat away from your precious camp.

Left that same camp standing.

"I need to get into that facility."

"Why?"

"It has information I need."

"That facility is being cleared out by the Council now. Everything in it belongs to us. For the common good."

"I just want some maps from the inside."

"No."

She said it with finality.

"No?"

"Did I stutter?"

Her eyes flashed and I could see the hint of insanity in them.

"Why did you drug me?"

"You're a test."

"A test?"

"A test."

Was she going to tell me what kind of test?

"Are you testing my kids?"

The gurgle again, this time stronger.

Something must have crossed my face because two of the Colonels lifted their rifles and aimed.

I held up my hands to show them it was cool.

"We don't test children," she said. "We rescue them."

"They didn't need saving."

She sighed as if the weight of the world was on her meaty shoulders.

"You failed the test," she said. "We're turning you loose."

Finally, some good news.

20

CHAPTER TWENTY

Mags led me to the amphitheater where we first met.

The stands were empty now, except for a group of men who waited by the gate.

The gate led to the outside. I could see the forest beyond them as they pulled it open and stared at me.

"These men are going to escort you through the woods, out of our territory and make sure you never come back."

"Without my kids?"

"They're staying here where we can keep them safe."

I grunted.

The Colonel's inserted themselves between us and the men at the gate grabbed me by the arms.

They need not have bothered.

The drugs were still pulsing through me, I was still weak. I'm not sure what threat they thought I posed, but they weren't taking any chances.

"The Council has decided to let you go," Mags told me and wiggled her fingers in a childish wave good bye.

CHAPTER TWENTY

The men at the gate dragged me out and I almost cried out when it slammed closed and a bar fell across it with a loud metal clang.

They hustled me to the edge of the woods and along a beaten path.

I could smell the scent of smoke on the air, remnants of my fire maybe, or the forest fire they claimed I set.

I tried to watch the group around me, head swiveling between the men and the ground, my bare foot swishing under the Mylar blanket.

I'm not sure how I knew what they planned, but they weren't going to let me go.

Was it the sneer on the face of the one with long greasy hair?

The other with the hard looking grimace surrounded by pockmarks?

I didn't know.

All I knew was they were planning to take me out of range of the walls, and put one in my head.Go back and tell the kids Daddy is loose and fine and living on his own.

There are plans and machinations that people put into motion, when all most really want is just a live and let live world.

The six men trailing after me weren't going to let that happen.

They were going to live, and plan for me to die.

I wondered how long I had before they would make their move.

I wondered how I was going to get back in to rescue my children.

All the fog in my head swirled, while I stumbled along.

The six men bunched up, three in front, three behind.

It gave me an idea.

I tripped, and slowed down.

The three in front pulled ahead, and the next guy in line behind me reached out to grab my arm.

They should have tied me up.

Hell, they should have shot me in the hospital courtyard instead of thinking it was a good idea to get me away from the compound so no one would see their dirty work.

When he grabbed my arm, I twisted and pulled him off balance.

I thrust a fist into his throat, and shoved him back into the other two before he could scream.

Then I dashed through the trees, zigging and zagging as they yelled behind me.

It's funny what your mind thinks of as you're running through the woods being chased by armed madmen.

I remember reading an article about "prepping" or being prepared for the end of the world.

A lot of those guys had systems, and bunkers, full of weapons and food and plans to survive in a post-apocalyptic society.

This particular article focused on workouts that would help you survive Armageddon, though it didn't say one word about zombies, not even as a joke.

Something like, run a really long time to make sure your endurance is ready to go longer than the undead.

Nope, it skipped that part.

It talked about CrossFit exercises that would help you chop wood, and carry heavy game back to the bunker.

Which was smart.It also suggested going barefoot as often as possible to toughen up the soles of the feet.

Because one never knew when the shite was going to punch through the fan, and if you got caught with your shoes off, or worse yet, some enterprising bandits decided to abscond with your boots,being a shoeless joe wouldn't hamper the escape effort.

CHAPTER TWENTY

Maybe it wasn't so funny the article was on my mind as I winced my way through the woods.

My toes hurt.

My head hurt.

It all hurt, but the sharp twigs and angry rocks that gashed out for my tender footprints kept my mind on one thing.

Moving forward so the men after me couldn't catch up.

I just wished I'd paid more attention to their suggestion.

CHAPTER TWENTY ONE

We were two miles from the compound.

I could run it in twenty minutes and still have enough energy to climb wall, find the kids and bust them loose.

But I needed weapons.

There was six men between me and the walls and they all had guns.Seriously, no one watched Rambo and Die Hard growing up?

Six against one was nothing.

A cake walk.

I leaned against the rough back of the tree and smelled the wet leaves, trying to recall what happened in both.

I didn't have a tower to hide in or an elevator to climb in, nor did I hear a waterfall I could jump off of and escape into a deep pool of water.

All I heard were the men scrambling through the dead leaves as they hunted for me.

CHAPTER TWENTY ONE

Then I remembered.

Hunters don't look up.

I searched the ground around the tree and picked up a couple of pieces of dead branch. I slid it in the waist at my back and climbed the tree.

It was not as easy as I remembered from being a kid.

In the movies, the branch is just in reach and the hero grabs it, vaults to the crown of the tree like Tarzan in his glory days.

The lowest branch to this tree was fifteen feet off the ground.

I had to grip the trunk with my hands and forearms, use my feet to push up.

Then clench the inside of me feet against the circle of the bole and inch my arms up.

It did not feel good.

I made the branch and settled on it to catch my breath and tried to listen.

The men were closer, moving now toward the noise I made on the tree.

They would be here any minute.

I moved up two more limbs and wished for thicker foliage.

I wished for bark covered camo that would let me blend into the tree trunk.

I wished for a rifle and scope.

But all I had were six men hunting me and two short pieces of wood.

Stupid.

This was a stupid plan and I was a stupid man about to die.

My kids would be trapped inside the wall and never know.

They would think I chose to leave them, chose to abandon them.

There it was, the bubble of rage.

I fed the flames.

These men were trying to keep me from my kids.

They were trying to kill me.

I held out one of the sticks and tossed it into another tree past the one I was in.

It hit with a clack and fell with a clatter.

That brought two of the men toward me.

I could hear them approach, trying to be quiet, trying to sneak up on the noise and see what it was.

They reached the bottom of the tree I was in and did exactly what hunters the world over do.

They did not look up.

The only reason anyone looks up into a tree is if they're hunting squirrel or trying to shoot mistletoe out of the heights.

That's it. The rest of the time, hunters are searching the sight lines in the woods, which can get confusing and hypnotic with the different patterns created by branches, shadows, wind, and leaves.

The eye gets lazy and instead of trying to catalog everything, the vision goes sort of soft as the brain searches for anomalies.

Except they don't look up.

I tossed the second branch a few meters to the right and when it hit, they both turned.

I dropped on top of them.

I've lost a lot of weight since the Zpocalypse.

Part of it was starving a lot, but most of it was just sheer movement.

The amount of time I spent still on any given day was practically nil.

But one hundred and seventy pounds dropping twenty feet is a lot of mass to crash down on top of someone.

I hit with a foot on each of their shoulders.

It knocked me on my ass because there was no stable surface to land on, but it slammed the first guy into the tree trunk and sent his gun careening.

The second guy, long hair, folded under me with a cracked clavicle.

I tried to land a roll, and mostly succeeded, and made it to my feet.

Then I was on them.

I sent a foot into long hair's face and kept him occupied with a squirting nose.

The other guy was on his hands and knees crawling fast for his lost gun.

I landed a knee into the spine between his shoulder blades and sent him sprawling.

Then I grabbed his chin, planted both knees against his back and pulled until something cracked.

He stopped moving.

I should have grabbed his knife.

I should have grabbed the rifle.

But hindsight is always 20/20.

Instead I went for long hair and he screamed.It was more of a gurgle than a scream and it sprayed blood all over the moist leaves.

That brought the others running.

They shot, but couldn't hit me because it's tough to shoot straight when you're pounding through slippery leaves and aiming through trees.

I ran.

And left a trail they could follow.

Tracking is a skill I don't possess, but I do know if you want someone to trail you, turn over dirt and leaves.

Scrape bark off trees.

It's tough to do when you're trying to be obvious about it, and don't want the person tracking you to know you're being obvious.

The subtlety of it was lost with me.

All I knew is I wanted them after me once I put a little distance between us.

In the movies, they had time to build all sorts of booby traps learned in the jungles of Vietnam.

I think jumping from the tree was my one trick pony, but it took out two of them, plus one stayed behind to take care of long hair.

That's what I figured when he stopped screaming.

Either that or they killed him.

Three kept up with me.

It's easy to get lost in the woods.Terribly easy.It happened to me once when I was fourteen.

I was spending Christmas break with my Dad at the home he had in the country.

This sounds a lot fancier than it actually was.

The truth was my Dad lived in the woods, in a house owned by my grandfather.

We would go visit him on the weekends, and stay longer when school was out, even though we lived in the same town.

That time it snowed.

It didn't often snow in the small town where I lived, maybe once every other year.

This time it put almost eight inches on the ground.

I'd never been on a walk in the woods when it was white and quiet, the snow muffling very step.

CHAPTER TWENTY ONE

I bundled up and took off for a hike on the logging and three wheeler trails carved through the pine forest.

After an hour, I turned around and followed my footsteps back. Only they weren't my footsteps.

After three hours, I tried to pick one direction and kept walking.

At the end of the day I ended up almost thirty miles from my house when I stepped out on an ice covered highway. It was almost twilight, I was half frozen and terrified when a couple in a four wheel drive picked me up and drove me home.

Getting lost in the woods is easy.

I tried to think about that when I ran, because I needed to be able to find my way back to the compound.

I was thinking about it when I hit the edge of a shallow slope and pitched down a mud slicked side of creek. I slid to the bottom, tried to catch my breath and listened to the men chasing me.

They pounded through the leaves, clucking and whistling to each other as they tried to zero in on my position.

I sat up, felt the mud slurp around me and glanced at the lip of the bank where I tripped. It was an easy trail to follow.

But the creek had flooded in the past and carved a shallow depression under the hill.

It wasn't deep, just a few inches, but it was on the shadowed side of the creek, and I had an idea.

I slathered mud across my face and rolled over so it coated me.

Then I backed up into the dark ground under the lip of the creek.

It was a great hiding spot, but I saw a rock about the size of my fist next to the water and I yanked it up, just as someone stopped at the edge of the overhang and sent a shower of dead leaves across me.

I tried not to breath.

He didn't jump. He sat down, put both legs over the rim and jumped to splotch in front of me, studying the ground I had just wallowed on.

I listened for anyone close and decided to chance it.

He turned as I lunged from the mud, the two steps between us too tight for him to bring the gun to bear.

Then I beaned him with the rock.

He fell backwards into the creek and I was on top of him, pounding with the rock twice, three times.

I grabbed his rifle and pushed back toward the shadows, hoping to use his body as bait.

It worked. The next guy stopped at the top a few meters away. "Tom?"

He leaped down, fought for balance and recovered to kneel next to his buddy.

"Don't move," I said as he checked for vital signs.

He glanced over at me, and I'm not sure what he saw.

A mud covered monster holding a rifle at him from the shadows under a patch of ground. I might have been scared too.

He dropped his rifle and held up his hands.

"Don't kill me," he said in a loud voice. "Please."

His eyes flicked up.

I raised the rifle and sent a shot back over the edge and heard a yelp.

The guy down here with me threw himself forward to try to grab his rifle, but we were close.

I stepped out and slammed the butt into his chin, then went to check on the mewling man above.

Continued

CHAPTER TWENTY TWO

I tied them to the trees, the ones that were alive at least. I circled back to gather long hair and his crunched nose and his would be rescue party, stepping out of the shadows to take them by surprise.

I marched them back to join their buddies.

Four of them. Then I built a small fire made of twigs in a hole I scooped out of the ground, the tiny flames just enough warmth to work by.

I stripped them all of clothes, then washed the mud off me in the creek before putting on a little fashion show to find what fit.

They were not appreciative, or maybe they were quiet because of the sweaty socks I tied into their mouths.

All of their feet were smaller than mine, so I had to forego boots, but I doubled up on socks that weren't being chewed on at the moment. I sat on the ground in front of the fire, working over the actions of the rifles, checking the magazines and cleaning them as best I could with a scrap of cloth ripped from the dead man's shirt.

I finished and pulled a gag off the man closest to me.

"You killed Sid," one of them croaked through parched lips and I looked up to see which one.

He caught my eye and tried to hold it with his scared blue ones, the left twitching like an electric current ran under it from stress. "Where are my kids?"

"They're safe," he answered, then cackled. It sounded wet and phlegmy, like a smoker when they first wake up. "We kept 'em all good and safe. It's what we do with all the cattle."

Cattle. I didn't like the way it sounded and the way he said it. "Tell me." "Tell you what? There's nothing you can do," he crowed in a braggart's voice. "They'll send others to find us, too many for you to handle on your own and then you'll be dead."

"I thought your Council wanted me alive."

"Mags don't," said the braggart. "And the Colonel's work for Mags."

"Tell me more."

But he shut up after a glance at the others. I held up one of the rifles and let him watch me feed in the bullets. "You don't scare me," he sniffed. "You can kill me or let me live. I don't care much either way." A man who isn't afraid to die isn't scared easily. I knew from personal experience. But I also knew a secret. "There are worse things than death," I told him. He must not have liked the way I said it because I saw him gulp then, his Adam's apple bobbing up and down on his thin throat. Then he dug deep and bolstered his resolve. I almost admired him for that. Men and women have an infinite capacity for willpower, for being able to marshal reserves of strength that boggle the human mind. I'd seen it hundreds of times over, and we've all heard stories about people who do extraordinary things that seem superhuman. Scientists explain it is willpower and an adrenaline dump, the kind strong enough to let a mother lift a car to save her child, or a soldier like Audi Murphy to fight off a German battalion by himself after being wounded. This man had that much willpower. In another life, he could have been a hero too. But in this one, his will met mine. He didn't stand a chance.

23

CHAPTER TWENTY THREE

My ex wife had a habit that I hated. Whenever she wanted a chore done, or a lot of tasks knocked off the honey do list, she would pick a fight.

I would bottle up my anger and let it out through activity, which meant she learned how to selectively direct my behavior.

She didn't feel like doing the dishes? Pick a fight about money.

Wanted the yard work finished?

Start an argument about affection, or jealousy or any other tiny little thing.

She was an ace at it too with the ability to use digs and sarcasm in a single most annoying way.

The result was a lot of bad blood, a lot of housework and eventually a divorce.

After that, I was able to do some introspection.

Especially as I discovered long distance running. There is a

CHAPTER TWENTY THREE

lot of time to think during so many miles.

I realized that a lot of people did the same thing to me. My parents would make me angry to get a reaction.

My girlfriends would get fed up with how I bottled up emotions, and argue just to watch me feel something.

I went into professional environments to work where feelings were hidden, locked down and discouraged.

Because I didn't know how to have feelings.

I didn't know how to deal with them.

The zombie apocalypse may have been bad for the rest of the world, but at least it allowed me to get in touch with my gooey center.

Mine was made of rage.

Red hot molten lava of rage.

I'm not sure what caused it.

There was some abuse as a child, so maybe that messed me up. It certainly gave me a sense of justice and fairness about how the world should operate. Or maybe my depression era grandfather taught me to repress, to tough it up, to walk it off.

Showing emotion of any kind was weakness, and boys are not allowed to be weak.

Hell, maybe I did it.

I idolized strong men, the Rambo's, the Commando's and Die Hard heroes who were tough as nails and crapped bricks.

More likely it was a combination of things.

I bottled up the rage. I compacted it into a tiny little ball, a living swirling planet that orbited somewhere around my beltline.

Then I spent all of my adult life quashing it, keeping it quiet, holding it still.

Until one day, I didn't have to do that anymore.

Granted, the first time I let loose the rage, it was against the walking dead.

But since then I'd learned about a very valuable tool at my disposal.

Some people get crazy when they get angry.

I get cold. Calculated.

Some psyche major would have a field day with why.

Lucky for me, most of them were gone now, part of the Z herd I could decimate, and if any still survived, they were more concerned with eating than analyzing me.

Rage. Always simmering beneath the surface. Washing up like a tsunami and taking out

I turned it on for the four survivors and they talked.

They told me about the Council. About Mags. About the Colonels.

They told me about more Army bases and refugee camps, and if I would have asked for the Colonel's secret recipe they would have told me that too.

And when were done I let them slip into oblivion with a quick twist of the knife.

I didn't wash off in the creek again.

I wanted everyone in the compound to see the blood of their men on me. I even took trophies to show them what they were up against.

CHAPTER TWENTY FOUR

They told me all I needed to know.

How to get in.

Passwords.

Layout.

I moved back through the woods toward the compound, paralleling the path and moving slow.

I wanted to run, sprint back to the gate, break in and rescue the kids, but I was trying to play the caution card.

The prisoners also told me what I was up against.

And why Mags wanted the Fort.

They were out of supplies and growing desperate. The Colonels were her answer to growing unrest in her group. They played by Mafia rules, which is the strong got to do whatever they wanted to the weak.

They were fighting with another group of survivors, but none of the prisoners I took knew why.

My feelings were a little hurt that she didn't send better men than those to kill me. It was like she didn't think I was a threat.

I daydreamed a little about how I would make her rethink the position, but quelled it. My goal was to get in, get my trio and get gone.

Hopefully that fast, and with as little violence as possible.

I approached the gate I exited through and watched.

There were two guards on the sides, which was smart. They looked bored and tired.

Good for me.

I had the weapons my execution squad brought out with them, and from the trees I could take two shots and remove the guards.

But that would let the ones inside know I was coming.

It's tough to have a sneak attack when you can't be sneaky.

I needed a distraction.

A fire would help. The smoke would draw their attention. I could toss a couple of bullets into the flames and then move to another part of the tree line.

The shots would draw more people.

I considered hunting up a Z and leading it toward the gate, but they would shoot it, which would draw more attention.

Besides, I spent most of my time trying to avoid zombies.

Why would I hunt one up on purpose even if it was to use as bait.

Sometimes luck favors the bold.

Or in this case, the dumb luck.

A group of moving trucks rumbled up the road and stopped at the gate. There were six of them, with a pick up truck in the lead.

"Open up!" screamed the driver of the pick up as he leaned out of the open window.

CHAPTER TWENTY FOUR

One of the guards worked the mechanism and pushed the gate back while the second went to the passenger window.

"Did you get a good haul?"

"Better than good," the driver crowed.

I didn't listen to the rest. I scooted through the trees to the point closest to the last truck in line.

It was eighteen inches off the ground, and I'd only seen it done in movies, but it was my way in.

The guards moved to one side and waved the truck through.

I ran across the narrow open space and waited by the back to listen for a sound of alarm.

But all I heard was grumbling engines and the whine of gear as the heavily laden trucks moved forward.

I slid under the back of the truck and searched the undercarriage for a place to grip.

Parts moved, and the metal was hot, but I wedged my toes into the rear axle, and used shirtsleeves to pad my hands.

I lifted up as the truck took off, moving forward on the pressed gravel road.

The heat leeched through the cloth and started to hurt.

I shifted, and the butt of the rifle strapped to by back scraped against the rocks.

It almost knocked me off, and combined with the heat, made me cling by the tips of my fingers.

By the time we rolled through the gate, it was too much.

I dropped and let the truck rumble over me.

Luck held.

The gate was halfway closed, the guard watching his partner hidden behind the other side.

I rolled toward the shadow of the wall and waited, letting my hands cool off, trying to decide what to do next.

I was in.

CHAPTER TWENTY FIVE

Obi Wan made it look a lot easier than it was.

That's all I thought about as I crept around inside the compound and searched for sign of Tyler, Bem and the Boy. I didn't have Force mind control to wave off guards, and while I wasn't sure if these sharp shooters were as accurate as Stormtroopers, I wasn't ready to test it out.

It involved a lot of standing still.

And double checking a way to make sure it was clear.

Since there was dissension in the ranks, Mags had declared martial law, which kept most of the people in the compound locked in safe places. There were large yards within the rooms, areas the size of city parks with hurricane wire fences thrown around them, and locked with padlocks.

"For their safety," the last guy told me before I let him journey into the great beyond.

A cell within a cell. Or cells.

Which was good for me in a way.

It kept most of the ways clear.

And bad in that I didn't know which cell the kids were in.

"You're pretty good," said Mags from over my shoulder. "Better than I imagined."

So much for being sneaky.

She waited around the corner from me. I leaned against the side of the wall and tried to think of a way around it.

Or through it.

"We had a check in time for the boys I sent with you," she said.

I could hear her voice just on the other side. It sounded like she was leaning too, just a couple of people passing time.

"When they didn't come back, I sent trackers after."

"They found my handiwork?"

"Is that what you call it? No. They found your trail and followed you back here."

I nodded.

"Any of them going to come home?" she asked.

"Nope."

She sighed. It carried through the wall, a heavy sounding thing full of angst and a hint of frustration.

"It can be expected," she said after a moment. "You think you'll find your kids in here? That is what you're looking for, right?"

I didn't answer.

I didn't have to. She knew who I was searching for and the reason I came back.

Then I realized she was the distraction.

Mags pulled my own trick on me. Two of the Colonels stepped around the corner and into the hallway aiming their rifles at me.

I thought about fighting back for just a moment, taking one with me, maybe using the element of surprise to scare the other, make him jump and misfire.

But another stepped around from where Mags was talking and hiding, black barrel almost pressed into my face.

It was a classic move.

And when no one pulled the trigger, I figured they had something worse in mind.

Worse than taking me out to the woods and shooting me, which didn't work out so well for them the first time.

26

CHAPTER TWENTY SIX

Things break down faster in the South, I think. The heat and humidity, the relentless crawl of foliage, the frequent storms and perhaps there is something more.An Irish disposition to half assed construction. A ride the clock and get it done frame of mind when it came to building things. Those things didn't last long.Maybe it was a modern take on construction, since some houses built in the Victorian age still stood. Certainly not a Roman approach, since those bastards built viaducts and Parthenon's that stand still to this day.I was looking at a building and wondering if it would still be here in a thousand years. I was leaning my bet on the southside of twenty, if that.The windows were still intact, except for the top left corner on the front side.That was the side that faced the wind, the brick structure a brunt offense to the fast flowing breeze that angled off the River.That wind would drive in rain from the next storm, until a small puddle formed just on the edge of the building where the joints met at the floor.That water would seep in, and through the floor, flowing across the wood that held the joint together and rotting it with the heat.It would spread like a cancer across the interior of the building, made worse by snow, worse by freezing and thawing and more rain that followed, until a year from now, two years from now, part of the floor would collapse.The first sign of decay would signal the rapid decline of the rest.Twenty years from now, it might be a shell of a building. Maybe with a tree and wildflowers growing through the roof if they make it in through the first window, or the second when it breaks as it must.No, things do not last for long in the South.Except for hatred.And anger.As if the Irish and Indians and Africans there populated the area created sinkholes of despair and rage, pockets of bad energy that floated around like a fog among the trees.I was staring into the face of that rage right now.A red headed woman who towered over me by a foot glared down from a pedestal.No, literally it was a pedestal. She had coerced or forced minions to place a giant chair up on a dais so that she towered over the rest of us from the lofty position.Right now she was trying to decide if she should kill me.I could tell by the look in her eyes.I'd seen that look before, often after the Z plague hit, but a couple of times before from women who also wanted me dead.It was an itchy skin kind of feeling, but like a good meek prey under the watchful gaze of a predator, I just sat there and didn't scratch the itch.Trust me, scratching the itch would have made things worse.I almost told her to kill me.I almost wondered why she didn't just do it.It would be the smart thing to do. How many men had I cost her? She had to know I was going to keep coming, keep trying to free the kids.There were two moves here, kill me to eliminate the threat, or turn us loose and watch as we made tracks to points East.So why didn't she?I try to remind myself that people do not act according to logic most of the time. They act according to the logic they believe, which can make them an enigma to everyone else.I tried to be clear with everyone.I'm going to Arkansas to find my children.I did.I'm going to Georgia to find my youngest.I was.I needed information. I asked for it.If you got in my way, I killed you.Pretty cut and dried.I think if everyone lived their life like an open book, there would be far fewer problems in the world.Unless you counted the zombie plague as one huge problem, and the power grabs after as just another day at a new type of office.But one of her men was pointing his gun at the back of the Boy's head.Another held a pistol by his thigh, ready to point it at Bem.Berta smiled."Tell me what you want," I called out to her."I want you to leave.""Lady," I shook my head. "What the hell do you think I've been trying to do.""Just you," she purred.I clenched my fist so hard it almost cramped."Not without them."She made a small finger movement and the guy behind the Boy shoved him forward."We want you to leave too Dad."My stomach dropped and I studied his face.He had a good poker face, but the skin around his eyes was tight, smooth. He was holding onto a frozen mask, trying hard not to betray any emotion. I wasn't close enough to see his pupils, but it looked like fear.Bem stepped up beside him."Please Dad, just go. We want to stay here with them."I watched them for a moment, and glanced at Tyler."You too?"He nodded tightly."You see," said Mags as she gestured with your hand. "No one wants you here. You're a danger to us. To them. To yourself."My mind was racing as I tried to find the angle.Were the kid's brainwashed? Threatened?My eyes landed on Tyler's.He winked.One eye, slow.Maybe it was a sign. Maybe it was the wind.But I felt a surge of hope.And hoped it didn't show on my face. The thing about signals though is knowing what they meant. "Are they safe? Really safe?" I squared off on Mags and kept my face as still as I could. "They are." She stepped down from the stage, and I could feel the men around me shift. This was it, I thought.

This was where I get shot, or worse. With my kid's watching. She stalked toward me like a giant cat, long legs swishing her camouflage pants until she was close enough that only I could hear her. "You're thinking about a rescue again," she purred. "And you're wondering why I don't kill you now." I didn't nod. "You're going to do me a favor," she told me. "Do all of us a favor." "Don't come back?" I guessed. She snorted through her aquiline nose. "As if I could stop that," she said. "We've seen what you are capable of. My men have seen the results of what you have done. The fact that you are standing here in front of me is proof enough of your ability." She leaned slightly forward.

I could see a man over her shoulder lift his rifle up and aim. "We're having trouble with some of our citizens," Mags whispered. "You're going to use your skillset to retrieve them for me. And in exchange, I won't blow your children's brains out on your face and lock you up to live with it for a very long time." Voice steady. Calm.

A terrible promise that I knew she would make good on. Her eyes locked on mine and then she stepped back. "You've heard your children," she said so they could hear her. "They want you safe beyond our walls. I've decreed it," she turned to the men. "Escort him out." The guns stepped forward, blocking me from the stage, a wall of rifle barrels that pushed me back toward the doorway. "I am going to give you a day's supplies," Berta said as she smiled at the kids. "It's a kindness." Bem nodded, her lips a tight white line.

I watched her hand snake out and grasp the Boy's, holding it tight as the guns pushed me further away. They thought they were saving me.

They thought they were keeping me safe. Stupid noble kids. Where the hell did they get their ideas from? I bumped up against the edge of the door and stepped through backwards. My last glimpse of the kids, they were standing on the raised stage with Tyler behind them.

Maybe he winked again, but I couldn't be sure at this distance. Then the door rumbled closed and I was staring at blank metal.

CHAPTER TWENTY SEVEN

I didn't recognize the two men that brought the backpack.I suspected she had sent them partially as cannon fodder, two bodies she wasn't afraid to lose and if I wasn't holding my wraith in a tight rein, she would have been smart to think it could happen."Mags said there's a letter inside for you.""Great. A pen pal."I opened the pack and inspected the contents. One can of SPAM. No can opener. A six inch folding knife. And a letter.Enough food for one day.No weapons.I palmed the knife and eyed the two men.They had guns, two rifles and a pistol.Did she expect me to take their weapons?Would she retaliate against the kids if I killed a couple more of her citizens?My poker face slipped and both stepped back, the taller one putting distance between us.I grabbed the folded paper instead.It was instructions.That started with don't kill the men.And an address.Like I had GPS and could just look it up."Go," I told the men and almost laughed out loud as they sprinted away.I reread the instructions.They were simple.An address and just a few words.*Come back with them all, or your kids die.* I shouldered the pack, and started hoofing it.

I had to find the railroad or a road and get to a town. The needs were always the same. Weapons. Shelter. Food. And now a map. A map and a mission. My kids were still in danger and I was cast out. I let the rage simmer and broke out into a jog.

THE END

Thank you for reading Battlefield Z Bluegrass Zombie. If you liked it leave a review on Amazon or Goodreads. Authors love word of mouth. I appreciate you having some fun with me on this cross country romp.

Ready for More?

BATTLEFIELD Z OUTCAST Revenge. Rage. They kidnapped his children and sent him on a mission. Rescue their people and stop a madman, or his kids will pay the ultimate price. They turned him loose with nothing except his anger. But it's been enough fuel to drag him across a zombie wasteland before and nothing is going to stop him from saving Bem, the Boy and Bo Bistan. Not a million Z. Not a cult. Nothing.

Abandoned.

Alone.

And ready to hunt, Dad must save another group so he can protect his own before Mags makes good on her promise to turn his kids Z and make him kill them. Find out in BATTLEFIELD Z OUTCAST